THE TEXAS HILL COUNTRY MURDERS
BOOK 2

TREASURE & TREACHERY

KADY HINOJOSA

Visit the author's website at *www.kadyhinojosa.com*

Book Cover Design and Interior Formatting by 100Covers.

Editorial Services: Beth Dorward. Visit the editor's page on Reedsy at
https://reedsy.com/#/freelancers/beth-d

Paperback ISBN-13: 978-1-7354976-8-6

*For my husband, Jose, my rock,
my staunchest supporter, my favorite fan.*

*For my beta readers and ARC team, your input is
invaluable and I have the utmost respect for you
and all you do.*

*For my readers, your enthusiasm, honesty,
and support is appreciated,
more than I can say.*

Thank you.

Titles By Kady Hinojosa

THE TEXAS HILL COUNTRY MURDERS
Four Minutes of Darkness
Treasure & Treachery

THE MALI HOOPER THRILLERS
#HuntedLives
#JusticePrevails
#DanceFever

Join my mailing list and get monthly updates on new
releases, special deals, and more.
www.kadyhinojosa.com/s

Prologue

Late June 1878

Ian Smalley froze when he heard the hammer being pulled back on the gun that was now pressed against his temple.

"Where you been, Ian? We're in the final stages of planning the heist and you disappear overnight?"

William 'Billy' Miner, leader of the Miner gang, was a hard man. He'd stayed alive these past twenty-seven years because of his fast draw, quick wit, and suspicious mind. All came in handy when you were a thief. And Billy was one of the best. Whether stagecoach, bank, or train, Billy carefully planned his heists and had successfully stolen more than one hundred thousand in dollars and gold, most of which was hidden in various places around the hill country. He never killed for the sake of killin' but would if he had to.

Well known in these parts, as much for his heists as for his care in not hurting innocents, Billy stood just over five and a half feet tall and walked with a slight limp from landing wrong after jumping off a train. His golden hair, blue eyes, and ready smile made him a favorite with the ladies at the saloon.

The Texas Rangers had been on his trail for years, but they were always a few steps behind. No one knew where he lived or where to find him because he was always on the move. And they had no clue where or when he would hit next. There was no rhyme or reason to his actions and Billy enjoyed stymying them. He was even so bold one time as to rob a train that carried more than fifteen Rangers, or so the story goes.

Frank Houser, James Harper, and Ian Smalley were the other three members of his gang.

Frank was the oldest at twenty-nine and had been with Billy almost since the beginning, going on ten years now. He was a straight shooter, second only to Billy, and was all business. If he wasn't rolling a smoke, he was target shooting.

James was the youngest member of the gang and was a fun-loving, carefree sort, always laughing. His shot was true and his amiable manner and joking kept them laughing even in hard times. He grew up with Billy and was like a younger brother to him being two years his junior. They even looked similar with their golden hair and blue eyes, although James stood a couple inches above Billy.

James brought the fourth member, Ian Smalley, into the gang one year ago. Ian helped James awhile back, hiding him on his property when the daddy of a young lady he charmed into his bed came after him. He told Ian at the time that Daddy may have been upset but he left Rebecca smiling. Ian needed money, as his wife was sick and required medicine. He had moved his wife and son to Round Rock to be closer to the doctor who specialized in her ailment but his money had run out. He was desperate and begged James for help. James believed that he owed Ian and convinced Billy to let him in, a move Billy did not regret. Ian had proved to be a good addition. He could spot a Ranger a mile away and had been instrumental in their getaways on more than one occasion.

"I asked you where you been, Ian," growled Billy. His narrowed eyes never left Ian's face, which had paled considerably.

Ian's eyes shifted left and right and his breathing was erratic. "Billy, you were in town for your look-see so I told Jimmy that I had to buy medicine for Jenny and take it to her. You know how sick she is." The gang was holed up in a cabin about six miles southeast of Boerne, between Boerne and San Antonio. Ian looked at Billy, his pleading gaze willing Billy to understand. "It took me nearly half a day to get to San Antonio, buy the medicine and take it to her. The horse needed a rest so I spent the night with her and my son then left before sunup straight back here. I told James…"

James approached them from Billy's side and put his hand on the barrel of the gun lowering it. "Sakes alive, Billy. I spoke with Ian as he said, told him to get back early. You were late coming back from Boerne and I left early this morning to hunt for breakfast." He held up the two rabbits in his hand. "I didn't have a chance to tell you." He smacked Billy on his arm, his usual grin in place. "Don't kill the coosie. I'm hungry and want to eat." James laughed as he handed the rabbits to Ian and they turned and walked out of the barn.

Ian grumbled good-naturedly, "Quit calling me coosie, I ain't no chuck wagon cook."

Billy holstered his gun, staring after them until they walked inside the cabin and the door closed. Ian was more than their cook, of course, and had proven his loyalty and worth, but something didn't feel right to Billy. He absently pet his horse, who had popped his head out of his stall and was softly nickering.

Two hours later, Billy called everyone outside.

Frank placed his newly rolled cigarette in his mouth and lit it, taking a deep drag before blowing smoke out through his nose. "So we still go later today?" He always cut to the chase.

Billy looked at Frank then glanced at the other two and nodded. "A few things have changed, so listen up. I learned that the stagecoach arrives at three, no delays expected. We know that the gold is on it and will be taken to the bank's safe where it will stay overnight before they move it to Dallas tomorrow." He drew a crude map of the town in the dirt with a stick.

"How many Rangers will be with the gold?" James looked down at the map.

"Two on top, one inside."

James smacked Billy on his arm, grinning. "I can guess how you got that information." He made the hourglass shape of a woman with his hands. Everyone laughed. Billy just shook his head and cuffed James on the back of his head.

Ian, who had been silent since the confrontation with Billy, rubbed his chin. "How are we going to get into the vault? With that timer mechanism the newer vaults have, getting the combination from the manager won't help. Do we have any dynamite? We could make nitro and…"

"Absolutely not." Billy was emphatic. He had learned that by boiling dynamite and skimming the nitroglycerin off the top, you could drip the liquid into the door grooves to destroy a door. While he had dynamite that he used on occasion, he wasn't about to try something he'd never done before. Too risky.

This was a fairly new kind of vault. How did Ian know about it?

Billy rubbed his chin, staring at Ian. "Too risky and not enough time. How did you know about the new vaults, Ian?"

Ian's eyes narrowed. "I hear things."

Frank dropped his cigarette on the ground and crushed it with his boot heel. "So we're taking it before they put it in the vault."

Billy's gaze shifted toward Frank. "Once the stage stops, I figure they'll need a few minutes to get the gold off the coach. That's when we'll move in."

"Why don't we just leave now and rob the coach before it gets to Boerne?"

"I've been told there are two women and a child on the coach, Ian. I won't put their lives at risk. They'll be first off the coach before the Rangers move the gold." He gestured toward the map on the ground. "Frank, I want you in the saloon here..." Across the street from the bank was the town square. He pointed to a building on the right side of the town square and diagonal from the bank. "Park yourself with a drink next to the window at two-thirty."

James whined good-naturedly. "Why can't I park myself there? Frank has all the fun."

"That's exactly why you won't be there, Jimmy. This isn't about fun, you'll either have too much to drink or you'll let yourself get distracted by the lovely ladies."

"Ain't so." But Jimmy was smiling. Billy was likely right.

Billy pointed to the other side of the town square, two buildings down. "Ian, you'll be up here watching for the Rangers. You should have a good view of the road on the south end of town that turns onto Main Street and can alert us when the stage turns onto it."

Ian nodded.

"Jimmy and I will be here and here." He pointed to the town square for James and one of the buildings a few doors down from the bank for himself. "As soon as Ian gives the signal, I'll alert you both," he looked at Frank and James, "since you won't be in a position to see Ian. Ian and Jimmy will move here,…" he pointed to the corner of the road by the town square, "…and Frank and I will be here." Billy pointed to the corner of the building next to the bank.

"We go on my signal. Make sure your horses are nearby. We'll meet back here, each going a different way. Are we clear?" Everyone nodded. Billy looked at his time-piece. "It's twelve-fifteen now." He looked at Frank and Ian. "It takes an hour and a half to ride to Boerne. You need to leave in fifteen minutes. Jimmy and I will leave fifteen minutes after you. Everyone rides in separately and we need to be in place no later than two-thirty in case the stage arrives early."

Everyone silently went to their horses to saddle up and prepare their weapons. Billy always insisted that they wear the same clothing, blue jeans, black boots, black shirt, black bandana around their necks that they would use to cover their noses and mouths just before the heist, a long black jacket, and a black cowboy hat. Today was no exception.

As Billy watched Frank and Ian ride out, he reviewed the plan in his head one more time. It was a sound plan. And he believed what Lola had told him last night. She always said men tended to talk about anything and everything after ridin' her. And her information had always been reliable in the past.

He'd been with Lola more than any other, called her a friend because she'd saved his hide a time or two and he was always generous with his coin which she appreciated. As much as he was capable of trusting another, which wasn't much, he trusted her. When he was with her last night, she confirmed the stage's arrival time and had also found out how many Rangers would be on the stage. So why was he uneasy?

***

2:35 p.m.

Main Street in Boerne was bustling. Two young women strolled in the town square, parasols held above their heads to provide shade. Their heads were close together as they whispered to each other, covering their mouths with their hands as they giggled while sneaking glances at the young men lounging on some benches.

Horse-drawn carriages and flatbed trailers pulled by teams of horses slowly meandered down the street, wheels creaking and harnesses jingling along the way.

A few young boys played with a ball on the side of the street close to Billy, puffs of dust from the road flying up each time the ball bounced on the ground. They seemed unaware of the sweat dripping down their faces as their laughter filled the air. The heat of the day was oppressive due to the humidity but folks in Boerne were used to it and went on about their business.

Billy was the last to arrive, spying Frank and Jimmy when he rode in on Main Street from the north. He'd glimpsed Ian on the roof as he positioned himself on the corner of the building three doors down from the bank. Leaning against the wall in the shade, he lit a cigarette, swinging his eyes left and right, not missing anything, and keeping an eye on Ian throughout.

Ten minutes later, Ian looked toward the bank and waved his bandana above his head. Billy dropped his latest cigarette and crushed it beneath his boot heel, emitting a low whistle at the same time. He saw James look his way and stand up. When he glanced toward the saloon, he noted that Frank was already at the swinging saloon doors, ready to walk outside.

The next few minutes passed by in slow motion for Billy as he casually walked toward the bank, keeping his eyes on the road and listening for the stage. Stopping at the building next to the bank, Billy stood in the street between his horse, Rail, and another horse that was drinking water from a trough.

He didn't acknowledge Frank, who had walked across the street and was standing next to the wall. There was no mistaking the sound of the stage as it rumbled down Main Street. Both men tensed as they detected the clop-clop-clop of the horses' hooves and the occasional neighing of the four-horse team then watched as it approached. A quick glance across the street confirmed that Jimmy and Ian were also ready.

Lost in their own worlds of running errands and taking care of business, no one noticed the gang and they paid no attention to the stagecoach.

The stagecoach pulled up to the bank and the driver locked the wheel. It creaked and groaned when one of the men up top jumped down. The driver remained sitting. A stool was set below the door and then the Ranger opened it, assisting two women, one of whom was holding a baby, off the stage.

It was at that precise moment that Billy signaled his team to move in. They all slipped their bandanas over their noses and mouths, drew their guns, and rushed toward the stage.

In the split second they began to move forward, Billy's eyes grew wide as he looked at the two women for the first time. They were not walking away as one would expect. Glancing down, he noticed the boots they wore, not the dainty boots of delicate women. Rather, they were big, dusty, well-worn boots...the kind worn by Rangers.

"Trap!" he shouted.

Chaos ensued.

James, who was about to round the back of the stage on the south side of the street skidded to a stop.

A man, who had stepped out of the bank with his wife, took in the scene and shoved her back inside as she screamed. He followed her in, slamming the door behind him.

The young boys playing ball raced away, kicking up dust as they ran. The business next to the bank closed its doors and pulled down the shades on the windows, as did other businesses.

Frank stepped next to Billy and raised his gun just as the Ranger on top of the stage fired his rifle, shooting him in the chest. As Frank fell back, Billy shifted to the side and fired a shot over his horse, nailing the Ranger between the eyes. Without pausing, he turned his weapon on the Ranger who had initially set the stool, then ducked while holding Rail's bridle, as he was now nervously stamping his hooves.

The 'baby' was actually a pair of guns that the two 'women' grabbed. The baby blanket floated to the ground unheeded as the 'woman' Ranger nearest to the rear of the stage rounded the corner, stopping short when he saw James aim his weapon and fire. He was dead before he hit the ground. After firing, James stayed on the outside of the stage and moved toward the front. The second 'woman' Ranger jumped into the stage and fired out the window hitting James in his gut. James groaned and, clutching his side with one hand, fired toward the stage as he stumbled to the rear of it taking refuge behind a water trough just beyond.

"Billy, I'm hit, I'm hit," James shouted.

"Hold tight, Jimmy."

The Ranger in the stage opened the street side door and jumped out. The clink of his spurs alerted Billy, who fired a couple of rounds at the stage. Jimmy did as well.

"There's nowhere to go, Billy, and more Rangers are on their way. They should be here any minute."

Billy peeked below Rail's head, looking toward the water trough where James was hiding. Cursing under his breath, he reloaded his gun as he assessed the situation.

Untying the lead, he grabbed the reins and quickly led Rail onto the wooden sidewalk between the bank and the stage. He paused long enough to fire a shot under the stage, hitting the Ranger in his calf. As the Ranger fell, Billy fired another shot hitting the Ranger in his mid-section before running with the horse to the trough. He pulled James up, then helped him onto the back of the horse, climbing up behind him.

Just as he set his heels into the sides of the horse, the pop of a gunshot reached his ears a split second before a bullet tore into his upper back. He grunted and fell forward against James before both rocked backward as the horse surged ahead and shot down a side street.

James held the pommel of the saddle with one hand and his side with the other. Blood oozed between his fingers that were already drenched with blood. He was gasping for breath and groaned every time Billy turned directions. Billy gritted his teeth against the pain as he wove through town before making his way south. He had no idea where the additional Rangers were coming from, so he stayed away from the busier streets.

They hadn't traveled more than a couple of miles when James put his hand over the hand of Billy's that held the reins.

"No more. Can't go no more."

Billy immediately slowed Rail to a walk and assessed their surroundings. They were on a trail between trees and bushes. In the distance, Billy eyed a small ranch and made his way there. Coming up on the back side of a barn, he stopped.

"Hold on Jimmy. Let me check things out."

He limped to the side of the barn and looked toward the main house. There was no movement at the house and the field beyond was empty as well. Billy turned back and slowly opened the barn door, gun drawn. As it creaked open, Billy peeked inside. It was all quiet. He opened the door further and led Rail over to some hay, grimacing. His upper back was on fire.

He pulled James down and laid him gently on the hay. Dropping next to him, he groaned. "What a pair we are, eh Jimmy?" He paused, trying to catch his breath. "No one else I'd rather be with at the end." Billy coughed, then closed his eyes.

Chapter 1

October 2024

"Mama, Mama, Mama!"

Claire St. John looked up from her computer, smiling when she spotted her two-year old son, Eddie. He was standing in his playpen, hands holding onto the side while his chubby little body bounced up and down. She always kept his playpen in her office for those days when he didn't go to day care. Today was one of those days.

He'd woken up cranky and with a stuffy nose. While he didn't have a fever, she kept him with her. She only had two clients today so she knew he wouldn't disrupt her meetings. Well, not too much anyway.

Her office space consisted of a reception area, her office, and a restroom. It was located in the old downtown area on Main Street. A cute little vintage boutique had closed after COVID so she was able to rent it dirt cheap. She loved the location especially because her favorite bistro, Barkley's Bistro, was right across the street.

Pushing back from the desk, she stood and walked over to him. "Look who's awake!" She laughed when he gurgled and raised his arms. "And feeling better too, by the sound of it." Claire picked him up and hugged him close breathing in his scent. He still had that baby smell that she loved so much.

Claire and her husband, Michael, had tried for years to get pregnant. After three miscarriages in five years, they both kind of gave up...on having kids as well as their marriage.

Born and raised in California, Claire was majoring in finance management at California Polytechnic University in San Luis Obispo with a minor in real estate finance when she met Michael. He was a guest speaker for a real estate financial class she was taking. He worked for a national real estate development firm in Dallas, a guru of sorts specializing in land and property development.

She was fascinated by the man as well as the topic so she'd approached him after class to ask some questions. That led to dinner followed by the most mind-blowing sex she'd ever had and they'd been together ever since. His thirty-one years to her nineteen didn't matter. They were like two peas in a pod. He flew to California at least twice a month and she went to Texas whenever she could. They couldn't get enough of each other and married the following year when she graduated early at the age of twenty.

The realities of marriage took their toll. Michael was in demand and busier than ever working on a multi-state real estate project that quite often took him to cities in Colorado, Oklahoma, New Mexico, and toward the end of his life to smaller towns like Boerne. And she was making a name for herself at a large financial firm in downtown Dallas.

She was completely shocked when, at twenty-six, she discovered that she was almost four months pregnant.

Her previous miscarriages had occurred in the first trimester so she was cautiously optimistic that she'd be able to carry this baby to term.

Michael had been in Boerne for a month and would be there for two more months, so she gave him the news via FaceTime. He couldn't cover his lack of enthusiasm and didn't try, and she couldn't hide her disappointment. He explained that life was just so busy for them both right now but added that they'd make it work.

She offered to go to Boerne for the weekend, but he'd told her that an expected sale was going sideways and to stay home. They only spoke two more times until he returned home more than two months later. A month after that he was dead, killed in a car accident.

Bouncing her son up and down and listening to his laughter made everything she'd gone through worthwhile. She sang his favorite song, "Jesus Loves Me," on her way to the refrigerator and pulled out his bottle along with a baggie of grapes she'd cut in half last night. Situating him in his portable high chair, she placed both items on the tray in front him, smiling when he picked up the bottle and eagerly drank the water. She grabbed a few toys from the playpen for him as well.

"There you go, cutie!" She bent down and kissed his forehead then returned to her work.

Being an independent financial advisor and having the flexibility to do things like keeping her son at her office if needed, was critical for her as a single mom. She was in her final trimester when Michael was killed and she couldn't afford to stay in the house.

She needed help so when her aunt offered, Claire sold the house in Dallas and moved to San Antonio.

Living with her aunt and having that support was a godsend. Right after Eddie was born, Claire started her own firm and built up a nice list of clients. Most had stayed with her when she moved to Boerne. But she'd have made the move even if she'd lost all her clients.

Raising her son in the small town of Boerne was important to her and it reminded her of small-town life in Twain Harte, California, where she grew up, which was an unexpected perk. Twain Harte was a quaint mountain town amid towering pines named for authors Mark Twain and Bret Harte.

When her phone rang she absently picked it up, still focused on her computer screen.

"Good morning, Claire St. John."

"Hi Claire, it's Grace."

With a smile, Claire leaned back in her chair. Grace Strong had become a good friend after Claire had hired her a few years back to work on her website. She had added some critical functionality that had helped Claire's business grow three-fold and she was currently working on a new project for Claire.

"Grace, hello. Your ears must have been burning because I was planning to call you today. How are you and how is Jo?" JoAnne was Grace's fifteen-year-old daughter and had taken care of Eddie off and on throughout the summer.

After the Ephesian Church of the Texas Hill Country closed six months ago, Jo had been looking for some part-time work to stay busy. She used to volunteer at the church helping with the foster children so she was the perfect babysitter. Even after all this time, Claire still couldn't believe everything that had happened during the eclipse and how Pastor John had been trafficking most of those kids.

"So that's why they were on fire." Grace laughed. "Jo is fantastic. Volleyball is in full swing and she's the varsity captain this year, as you know, so between that and her school work she's very busy. She has a boyfriend too, a senior."

"That warms my heart. How are you and Ethan?"

"I thought you'd never ask." Grace paused. "Ethan and I are engaged!"

Claire squealed. "OMG! Congratulations! When did he ask, how did he ask, I want all the details!"

"He asked me two nights ago but not before he asked Jo for permission."

"How sweet is that!"

"He told me that she was like 'it's about time dude, we've only been living here for two months!' before giving him a big hug."

Claire and Grace both laughed.

"We were relaxing on the sofa watching a Hallmark movie if you can believe it."

Claire giggled. "No, really? Oh, Ethan's going to get an earful the next time I see him."

"Right in the middle of the movie, he excused himself for a minute and when he returned he got down on one knee and asked. He said that he was trying to figure out the right time and watching a rom-com with his gal was the perfect time."

"Oh, Grace. I'm so happy for you two!"

"Thanks Claire. We're thrilled! We told Kent yesterday. He said the same thing Jo said, that it was about time. He's still keeping to himself, looks like a lost puppy."

Claire sighed. She and Kent Adams had dated for a couple of months after the eclipse but things hadn't worked out. She grabbed her cigarettes and walked to the door at the back of her office that led outside. Standing there with the door open so she could keep an eye on Eddie, she lit up and took a deep drag. She exhaled through her nose. "That's too bad," was her clipped reply.

"Oh shoot. I'm sorry I brought him up, Claire. I know you have your reasons and it's none of my business. I just want you to be happy." She quickly changed the subject. "Hey, I have the drafts of the login flow for your website. With the registration piece complete this is our next step."

"Oh good. That's what I wanted to talk with you about. And I want to thank you again for taking this entire functionality super slow, piece by piece. It's easier for me to wrap my head around it all by just thinking about one element at a time."

"It's actually easier to break this large project into small pieces. We can develop each piece, test them, and then test pieces that we put together until the entire project is done."

"You're making it very easy for me." Claire watched the sliver of smoke rise from her cigarette. "How does Monday look? We can meet at the Bistro for lunch, then you can come to the office afterward."

"That's perfect. How about noon?"

"Sounds good. Thanks. And Grace? I am happy. Enjoy your weekend."

"You too, Claire."

After she hung up, she looked up at the sky, enjoying the calming effect of the cigarette, reflecting on what might have been.

Chapter 2

JUST AFTER LUNCH, THE LITTLE BELL on the front door jingled and squeaked as it opened.

"Yoo hoo? Claire dear, are you here?" A head with the wildest mop of white hair peeked around the corner of her office door, which was slightly ajar.

"William!" Claire stood and rushed to the door to assist William into his seat. His fastest walk was a slow shuffle so it was easy for her to reach him before he finished walking through the door.

William Miner was an old codger. In his early eighties, he was a smidgen taller than Claire's five foot four inches, although he stooped a little. He had the kindest brown eyes she'd ever seen. That, combined with his wild hair, made Claire think of Albert Einstein every time she saw him.

William had been coming to her office since right after she first opened. He invested with her periodically, but he came to her office once or twice a week to chat, a little about investments and a lot about life. Claire loved it. Her relationship with him had developed more into a father-daughter one, and she cherished her time with him.

So did her son.

As soon as Eddie spotted William, he started bouncing up and down in his high chair, clapping his hands, and squealing. His water bottle rolled to the ground and the remaining grapes on the tray scattered everywhere. "Papa, Papa, Papa!"

William's eyes lit up. "I was hoping Jack would be here." William had never married and had no children. In fact, he had no close relatives at all, so it had quickly become apparent to Claire that he'd taken them under his wing.

Outside of official business, like daycare and doctors, William was the only person who called her son by his first name, named after Michael's father. But to her, he was Eddie. Edward was his middle name, just like her dad's.

Claire laughed as she picked Eddie up and took him to William. "You got lucky. He woke up this morning with a stuffy nose and he was a little cranky so he stayed with me." She handed the wiggling toddler over.

"Ooof. This little fella ain't so little anymore." He made goo-goo eyes at Eddie as he bounced him on his knee. "It won't be long before I won't be able to hold him." This was said as Eddie, now content with William's presence, wriggled off his knee and explored the room.

"I'm in the same boat, William. He's getting so big." She paused. "How are you? Did you take care of your will, as we discussed a couple of months ago?" During one of their visits, Claire was appalled to learn he had no will. When he told her he had no close relatives, she explained that having a will would ensure that his property and assets were taken care of the way he wanted.

"I met with the lawyer, and it's signed and sealed. Set up one of them trusts too. Those dang developers won't get a square inch of my property."

"Developers?"

"Yeah, some hoity-toity large real estate firm wants my land. They've been harassing me for a couple of years now."

"Why do they want it so bad? Have they told you what they want to do with it?"

"They said that growth is moving north toward Sisterdale and that my property was in a prime location to build a large park with shops and restaurants." He sniffed. "I don't believe a word those yellow-belly liars say. Who is going to go shopping and eat a meal in the middle of nowhere?"

"Hmmm, and there isn't any way to make them stop?"

William shook his head. "They're greedy bastards. They bought Jess Tucker's property to my left and Hank Johnson's property to my right a couple years back, just a few weeks apart as I recall. Some young pup stuck around for awhile after that to try to change my mind but I held fast. They need my land to fully develop the area. Haven't heard much from them since that time but they're still interested. They call now and then. I keep telling them I ain't selling but they keep trying."

Claire sat straight up, her frown deepening as she listened to him. "William, are you taking precautions? I mean, this could get ugly."

He waved his hand dismissively. "Nah, they're not going to hurt me. That would be too obvious. Besides, I've got good people working for me. We already patrol the property regularly with drones" He reached over to pat her hand. "And I have you to thank for getting on me about a will. My lawyer has assured me that between the will and the trust,. there's no way they can get my land."

Claire relaxed. "Well that makes me feel better."

"Don't you worry about me." He leaned back in his chair. "So are you coming over for our weekly Sunday dinner?"

"Mama, ball." Eddie was standing on the outside of his playpen, holding on to the netting with one hand and pointing at a red ball inside.

Pushing back her chair, Claire stood and walked over to Eddie. He giggled when she lifted him high over her head and kissed his belly before placing him inside the playpen. "Here you go, Sweetie."

Returning to her desk, she grimaced. "We can't on Sunday, William. The church is putting on an afternoon of Halloween fun for kids so I'm taking him there. How about Wednesday evening? It's the day before Halloween and I can bring Eddie in his costume. He's going to be the cutest bumblebee you've ever seen."

"I like that idea. After dinner, I want to show you something of my great-grandfather's."

"You're talking about Billy Miner, right? I'm intrigued."

"You remember."

"Of course I do. I remember all our conversations. He was quite the scoundrel. And didn't you say he left a treasure somewhere?"

William nodded. "A lot of people have looked for that treasure over the years. We'll talk more about it on Wednesday when I show you the trunk." He wiggled his eyebrows and grinned.

"William Miner, you are as much of a scoundrel as your great-granddaddy leaving my curiosity piqued like this." She laughed as she and William stood and walked to the office door.

Opening it the rest of the way, Claire stopped short. Her hand flew to her chest and she gasped when she came nose to nose with Lenny Garcia who was standing right outside the door. He took two quick steps back and moved to the side.

Her body sagged in relief. "Oh, hi Lenny. You startled me. How long have you been here?" She waved a hand and continued before he replied. "No matter. You're a bit early but have a seat in my office. I'll be right with you."

Lenny was a new client of Claire's. This was their third appointment. Standing just under six feet tall, his greasy black hair was tied in a ponytail and he was wearing greasy jeans and a long-sleeved denim shirt. He always reeked of cigarette smoke. With his long, pointy nose and shifty eyes, he looked like a weasel, but he was pleasant enough.

Lenny rubbed his hands together. "Thanks Ms. St. John." He inched past William before disappearing into Claire's office.

Claire walked William to the front door.

William looked at Claire and nodded toward her office, a question in his eyes.

"Lenny? He's a new client, a nice man and all alone," she whispered. "But thanks for your concern."

"Looks shifty to me. You watch out for him." He squeezed her hand as he walked by. "Until Wednesday, five o'clock. I'll take care of dinner."

"We look forward to it."

As Claire closed the front door, she paused and wondered how she didn't realize that Lenny had entered the foyer. The bell didn't ring. *How long had he been there and was he listening to my private conversation?*

She gave herself a mental shake. William was putting ideas in her head. Regardless, she made a mental note to take more care of her client's privacy. She walked into her office and sat down at her desk. "How have you been, Lenny?"

***

With no other appointments after Lenny left, Claire closed early. She locked the front door, turned off the lights in the reception area then went into her office. Eddie had just woken from a nap and was still lying in the playpen rubbing his eyes. Claire packed up her computer before walking over to Eddie and lifting him into her arms. He wrapped his chubby arms around her neck as she walked out the back door. After locking it, she climbed the iron stairs on the right that led to her one-bedroom apartment above her office.

After Michael died, she was shocked to discover that he'd maxed out his platinum credit card. The only argument they ever had was when he obtained that card. In her opinion, the annual fee was too high, as was the credit limit. He said he needed it for business and not to worry. As a result of his spending, she could barely pay off the mortgage and the card when she sold the house.

She berated herself for not paying more attention when Michael was alive, and she was forever grateful to her aunt for taking Eddie and her in and giving her time to sort things out so she could start anew. Moving to Boerne was that fresh start, close enough to her aunt in San Antonio but on her own. Thankfully, she had not needed to tap into her retirement account from the firm in Dallas.

One reason she rented the space on Main Street was because it included the apartment. She hoped to continue saving money so she could buy a little house for them. She estimated it would take twelve to eighteen months to save enough money for a down payment if she was careful.

Eddie squirmed in her arms. "Hungy Mama."

"I know, Sweetheart." Claire kissed his forehead and set him down in the living room where his blocks were scattered. "Build Mama a house while she makes you a snack. It's a little too early for dinner." She smiled when Eddie grabbed a red block and put the corner into his mouth before reaching for another.

She set her computer bag on the corner of her beige sofa and walked into the kitchen. She paused to look around and realized how little she needed. This apartment was vastly different from the forty-two-hundred square foot home in Dallas. The kitchen, dining nook, and living room were all one open space in the apartment.

The kitchen had a refrigerator, cabinets, a range with a gas stove top that she loved, a small pantry on the back wall, and an island where the sink and dishwasher were located. There was no microwave, but she didn't mind. Standing at the island, the dining nook was to her left and had a cute light brown banquette that formed an L against the wall on one side and under the window on the other. The living room was beyond the island with a window looking out on to Main Street below.

All of that, plus the oak ceiling beams and the antique lamps in the room, reminded her of days gone by. Their bedroom and the one bathroom had a similar look although she'd accented the browns and beiges with a pale blue comforter and accessories. It was home.

Eddie interrupted her musings when he waddled over to her and patted her on her leg. "Hungy!"

Lifting him into her arms, she carried him to the dining nook and placed him in his booster seat. His little face scrunched up, turning from pink to red. Crocodile tears ran down his cheeks as he slapped his hands on the table.

"Hang on, Sweetheart. I'll have your snack ready in just a minute." Turning to the refrigerator, she pulled out turkey slices, applesauce and milk. After pouring milk into his sippy cup, she handed it to him before returning to the island.

Eddie took a sip of the milk then threw the cup onto the floor, crying again.

She cut the turkey into bite size pieces, grabbed a spoon for the applesauce and placed everything on the table in front of his booster seat.

The tears evaporated as he grabbed a piece of turkey and shoved it into his mouth. Grace chuckled as she sat next to him. Dipping the spoon into the applesauce, she put the spoon next to his mouth. "Hmmmm. Yummy applesauce."

He made a face and turned his head to the side.

"Sweetie, you love applesauce." She made airplane noises as she spun the spoon in all directions ending at his mouth.

Eddie was unimpressed and pressed his lips together.

Claire sighed. "Okay, I'll eat it then."

As she ate the applesauce, Eddie finished the turkey, babbling the entire time.

Evenings with her son were Claire's favorite part of each day. She cherished the simplicity—dinner, bathing (which typically drenched Claire to Eddie's delight), and reading a bedtime story before putting him to bed. Once he was asleep, she'd pull out her computer and work until ten o'clock when she'd watch the news before turning in for the night.

Tonight was no different, except Claire opted to read instead of work and she soon lost herself in the historical romance.

Chapter 3

AT FIVE MINUTES TO TWELVE ON Monday, Claire walked into Barkley's Bistro. Grace had introduced her to the bistro a few months ago and she loved going there.

The bistro was owned by Margaret Anderson, a firecracker and dynamo despite her petite size and age. She spoke her mind, not caring who heard or who she might offend. At nearly ninety years old, she claimed she'd earned the right.

The bistro was a family business and she was a teenager when she first began working there, taking over for her father when he retired. Originally a saloon back in the late eighteen-hundreds, it still sported the original wooden bar, although a large mirror framed by ornate woodwork now graced the wall behind the bar instead of simple shelves that once held liquor. The foot rails and spittoons in front of the bar had long since been removed. Booths lined the wall opposite the bar and tables were in the middle. A back room offered more seating although the room was more contemporary in design.

Maggie's son ran the business now and her grandson was the chef who only bought locally-sourced produce and meat, creating eclectic dishes that the locals loved.

Serving breakfast and lunch with brunch on Sundays, it was always packed.

"Morning Maggie." Claire waved to the older woman, who still helped out at the bistro from time to time. Slightly stooped and weighing no more than one hundred pounds soaking wet, Maggie had frizzy white hair that was thinning on the top.

"Grace is in back, honey, and you may as well say afternoon although these old bones are telling me it should be about midnight considering how long I've been here."

Claire laughed. "I don't want to hear it. You've got more energy than everyone in this room combined."

"Oh you." Maggie cackled. "Go on back before you have me blushing."

Claire shook her head as she walked to the back room. Spotting Grace, she wove around the tables, waving to a couple a few tables away before smiling at Grace as she sat down.

"Maggie's in rare form today."

Claire giggled. "I honestly don't know how she does it. I get tired just watching her." She leaned forward and held out her hand palm up. "Let me see it, soon-to-be-Mrs. Marshall."

Grace blushed then placed her left hand in Claire's.

"It's beautiful! Wow! Ethan did good." Claire squeezed her hand before releasing it.

Grace held her hand up to admire the ring. "I love it." She placed her hand back in her lap. "I love your hair by the way. When did you add the auburn highlights?"

"Thanks. About two weeks ago. My brown hair was just so mousy looking, I needed something to make it pop."

"You certainly did that. It looks great." Grace took a sip of water. "How's Eddie?"

Claire picked up the menu that was on the table. "He had a bit of a stuffy nose so I kept him with me on Friday. But all is well today and he happily ran to his friends at daycare when I dropped him off this morning."

"I'm glad that's working out. Jo loved taking care of him during the summer but with school starting and Jo's commitments…"

"Grace, you don't have to apologize for Jo not being available to babysit. School is top priority and I'm delighted she's doing so well. Between daycare, keeping him with me on occasion, and with Jackie's help, I've got it covered."

Grace's eye crinkled as she smiled her thanks. "Speak of the devil…" She looked past Claire and waved. "Hey Jackie."

Jackie Baker was the assistant to the principal at Boerne Middle School and when she wasn't working at the school she helped Claire with Eddie as needed. Short and stocky and about twenty pounds overweight, she reminded Claire of Monica on *Friends* during her high school years. She even had black shoulder-length hair like Monica, although she kept it hidden beneath a beanie cap most of the time. The main difference was that Monica was cheerful despite being overweight whereas Jackie was quiet and very serious. But she took good care of Eddie for which Claire was grateful.

"Why don't you join us? We were just getting ready to order." Claire moved her bag off the chair next to her.

"Are you sure? I don't want to interrupt and I was going to grab a sandwich and head back to the school. I just left the doctor's office."

Claire patted the chair. "Sit with us until your sandwich is ready."

"Thanks." Jackie pulled out the chair and sat down.

"Is everything all right?"

Jackie looked over at Grace. "The doctor's appointment? Just a regular check up."

Gina, the waitress, interrupted them. "Hi y'all. Are you ready to order or do you need a few minutes?"

They spent the next few minutes placing their orders and catching up. When their orders were delivered, Claire and Grace convinced Jackie to stay and eat her sandwich with them.

Maggie joined them as well and nibbled on a celery stick while they ate. "Did I see William walk into your office last Friday?"

"Yes. He stops by regularly to visit or invest. Yesterday was just a visit."

Lips tightening, Jackie crossed her arms. "Seems kind of inconsiderate to interrupt your work like that."

Claire looked at her. "Not at all. I love his visits." She turned to look at Grace, who was frowning. "I'm sure he gets lonely. As a matter of fact, we're headed over to his place on Wednesday for dinner." A flash of anger passed through Jackie's eyes. "And Eddie will be in his bumblebee costume to show him."

"How nice," Jackie stated, a little stiffly.

Grace's eyes narrowed as she glanced at Jackie before she returning her attention to Claire. "William will love that."

"He's been telling me about his great-grandfather, Billy Miner. A real outlaw! He robbed stagecoaches and banks, was quite the charmer too, evidently."

Maggie was shaking her head before Claire finished. "That old coot is filling your head with falsehoods. Billy Miner couldn't be his great-grandfather because he died in a shoot-out and he didn't have a wife or any kids."

Claire frowned. "Are you sure?"

"He's just pulling your leg." Maggie grimaced. "He's been telling that falsehood for years. No one listens to him."

Grace tilted her head. "Really? He doesn't seem like the kind of man to do that."

Claire nodded in agreement.

"People have been looking for that treasure for years. It's spread all throughout the hill country." Jackie piped in.

"Not according to William. He said Billy collected all the loot and hid it in one place. He's going to show me a trunk that supposedly belonged to Billy."

"Hmmmm…well, don't believe everything you're told." Maggie pushed back the chair she was sitting in and stood up. "I've got to get back at it. Don't be fooled by William and his stories, Claire. And do that google thing to look up Billy Miner. You'll see what I'm talking about." She walked away without another word.

The three women stared after her.

"I hope I didn't anger her," stated Claire.

Grace shook her head. "She's just being her usual outspoken self."

Claire sighed. "We'd better head over to the office. I have a three o'clock and want to allow plenty of time for us to talk about the project."

"I've got to get back to the school as well," added Jackie. "Thanks for including me. This was much more enjoyable than eating at my desk."

All three stood and headed out of the bistro.

Later that night, Claire googled Billy Miner and read about his life. What caught her attention, however, was that his mother insisted that the man buried was not her son.

***

Late June 1878

"It hurts, Billy."

Billy opened his eyes, groaning as he struggled to sit up. "Let me take a look." James moved his hand and Billy pulled back his shirt. The bullet had hit his gut. Billy cursed.

"That good, huh?" James croaked out a laugh only to groan in pain.

Billy shook his head. "Always joking, eh Jimmy?" He pulled his bandana off and placed it over the wound, applying pressure. James gasped and closed his eyes, taking short, rapid breaths.

After a few moments, he turned his head and looked at Billy. "I know you been shot."

"Upper back on my right. Don't worry about me."

"Frank?"

Billy shook his head.

"Ian double-crossed us, Billy. When you gave the signal and I took off, I glanced back to make sure he was behind me. He was wearing a red bandana and was still by the wall."

"I know, Jimmy. Rest easy, save your strength."

"I'm sorry Billy. I brought him in, convinced you…" Tears slipped from the corners of his eyes toward his ears.

Billy was shaking his head. "This ain't your fault, Jimmy. I felt uneasy and should've paid heed."

James moved Billy's hand away. "I'm done fer, Billy, but you got a chance."

Alarm filled Billy's eyes. "I'm not leaving you. You're like my kid brother."

James shook his head. "I'm done fer and you know it." His eyes flicked up to Billy's hat. "Switch hats with me."

Billy frowned in confusion.

"They'll be searching for you. We look alike, close enough anyways. Take my hat and get out of here."

"Jimmy…"

"Let me do this, Billy. I'll die happy knowing you got away."

Billy tipped his head back and closed his eyes, swallowing a few times before looking down at James again.

"Go, and leave the front barn door open a crack. I want them to find me and they aren't the smartest lot, are they?" James grinned before coughing and gripping his body in pain.

Still Billy hesitated.

"Go. I'm getting the last laugh here, Billy. It's only fitting, right?" He grinned again.

Billy switched hats then squeezed Jimmy's shoulder before grimacing as he stood. He grabbed the reins of his horse and led him to the front of the barn. After sliding it open, he glanced back at Jimmy one last time then mounted the horse and rode away.

A short time later, as day was falling into night, four Rangers rode to the ranch. A witness had reported Billy and James heading this way. The owners of the ranch were on their way home when the Rangers caught up to them. The family was told to stay behind them until they inspected the property. In the few hours since the shooting, witnesses told them conflicting stories of where Billy Miner went, so the group of sixteen Rangers had split into four groups of four to investigate each lead.

As they rounded the curve and saw the house and barn, the Rangers stopped. The house looked quiet and uninhabited, but the barn door was open. The Ranger in charge motioned for two to go to the rear of the barn to make sure no one escaped while he and the fourth Ranger made their way to the front. Stopping by the corral, they dismounted and tied their horses to the rail. Guns drawn, they crept to the barn entrance and peeked in the door. Not seeing anything, they inched inside. A horse poked his head over the stall door startling the Rangers. Quickly moving out of the way, the Ranger in charge knocked over a bucket. Both men froze.

Hearing them, James opened his eyes, coughed and croaked out, "Over here. I'm Billy Miner."

Both men hustled over to James. The Ranger in charge squatted down beside him. "You and your gang killed four good men."

Taking shallow breaths, James managed a grin. "I saw two men and two women."

The Ranger sneered. "We're going to take you back into town so the doctor can patch you up just enough so that we can hang you." He turned his head to the side and spit onto the ground before standing up and turning to the other Ranger. "Get Hank and Simon and hook up their horses to this buggy here." It wasn't long before they loaded James into the buggy and headed back to town.

James managed to stay alive long enough to get to the doctor in Boerne but died a few short hours later.

William "Billy" Miner was pronounced dead and was buried in the town cemetery with a plain stone grave marker. The shoot-out and his death were in all the papers, and it was a long time before the town stopped talking about his escapades.

One year following his death, a frail-looking older woman arrived on the stagecoach. As soon as she put her things into her hotel room, she walked over to the sheriff's office.

"My name is Laura Miner. I'm William Miner's mother. I traveled from Boston because, despite the reprobate he was, he deserves a proper gravestone. I've brought it with me."

The sheriff stared at her in disbelief as soon as she introduced herself. "I, I, well, I'm pleased to meet you Mrs. Miner. I'm Sheriff Brown." He looked at his deputy. "Offer the lady a coffee."

"No thank you. Just tell me where my son was buried."

"Of course, of course." The sheriff was busy rummaging through papers in his desk. "I have the poster of your brother. It was required as proof when he was pronounced dead." He shuffled through papers that were in drawers. "Aah. Here it is." He handed her the poster.

At the top: "William 'Billy' Miner is dead"

At the bottom: "Died in Boerne, Texas, on June 29, 1878"

In between was a large picture.

Laura Miner took one look at the picture and declared, "This is not my son."

Chapter 4

THE DRIVE TO WILLIAM'S PLACE WAS relaxing for Claire, at least until she neared Pastor John's compound. Her shoulders scrunched up and her fingers tightened on the wheel even though he was dead and the compound was empty, with most buildings destroyed.

The city was trying to sell the property but there were no takers so far. It was impossible to miss. A six-foot wall ran the length of the property to the gold wrought iron eight-foot entrance gate which, when closed, formed a large cross. It was over-the-top in her opinion.

Claire had never been inside but Grace and Jo almost died there so she found herself slowing down as she passed it. She always did. Once beyond, she shook her shoulders and wiggled her fingers to relax.

William lived a few miles beyond Pastor John's compound, south of Sisterdale. There was an eight-foot stucco wall bordering the front of William's property, and the gate was a simple heavy-duty aluminum alloy that slid to the side. It opened automatically via remote or using a keypad at the entrance. Claire had her own code and used it.

His ranch was a working ranch and she passed multiple cows relaxing in the shade of various trees. Goats were munching on grass near the lake they passed. William's home, and the heartbeat of his operation, were just beyond the lake.

His house was a typical one-story ranch house with an extensive porch on all four sides. There were two rocking chairs to the right of the front door with a small wooden table in between them and a hanging double-wide wooden swing to the left. A mutt was sleeping at the top of the stairs leading to the front door. He didn't even lift his head when Claire drove up.

Eddie was bouncing up and down in his car seat. "Papa, Papa, Papa!"

Claire laughed as she unbuckled his seat belt. "Come on, Mr. Bumblebee. Let's go see Papa." As soon as she set him down, he ran to the stairs, navigating them one a time with Claire right behind him.

"Bear." Recognizing Eddie, the mutt's tail thumped on the ground and he lifted his head. Eddie stopped to pat him on the head.

William grinned. "Well who brought a bumblebee to my house and a cute one at that."

"Papa, Papa, Papa!" Eddie waddled up to him as fast as his costume would allow, giggling and lifting his arms.

Claire scooped him up and brought him close to William. "What does a bumblebee say, Eddie?"

"Bzzzzzzzzz."

William laughed, kissing Eddie on the cheek before stepping back to allow them inside. Bear followed.

Claire set Eddie down and walked with William into the living room. It was a large room with a long, dark brown leather sofa and leather loveseat sofas on either side that formed a U with a square wooden coffee table in the middle. The massive fireplace on the wall in front of the furniture was the central focus of the room and impossible to miss. Rocks surrounded it and went all the way to the ceiling. The fireplace itself was large enough that Eddie could walk inside standing up. An antler chandelier hung from the wooden beam that ran the length of the room.

"I hope you're not too hot with the fire I have going. It keeps these old bones warm."

Claire shook her head then walked up to the fire, passing Bear and Eddie who were sitting on the floor, and secured the screen which wasn't completely in front of the fire. "I welcome it." She stared up at the picture sitting on the mantle above. "I haven't seen this picture before."

"I knew you'd notice it." He joined her, his eyes crinkling with warmth. "It's a picture of my great-grandfather."

"This is Billy Miner?"

He nodded. "The best rendition I reckon. I found it in the attic when I was looking for the trunk." He pointed to a small trunk that was sitting next to the fireplace on the hearth.

"I can see where you got your good looks."

William hooted. "Oh go on."

The front doorbell rang and both turned toward it.

"I'll get the door, William." Claire walked over and opened it. Her eyes widened. "Jackie, hi!"

Jackie was holding two plastic bags by the handles. "Claire." Her eyes flicked past Claire to William, who was sitting on a loveseat talking to Bear and Eddie, before returning to Claire. "I've brought dinner."

"Oh my gosh, Jackie. Come inside." Claire opened the door wider.

Jackie edged past her. "Hi William. I've brought dinner." She glanced at Eddie sitting on the floor. "And who is that bumblebee sitting next to Bear?"

Eddie looked up when he heard his name. "Bzzzzzzzzz."

"Hello dear. You can set the bags on the kitchen counter." William stood and joined Jackie in the kitchen.

Claire had closed the door and was walking toward them. "I could have picked up dinner, William, and saved Jackie the trip."

"No, no. I said dinner was on me. Jackie has been a big help over this past year or so, right?" He looked at Jackie who nodded. "She gets my groceries and mails things for me. I really appreciate all you do, dear. You're a godsend." He reached over and squeezed her shoulder.

"I love to help, William."

"Wow! That is so nice, Jackie."

Jackie turned her gaze on Claire. "About the only thing William does on his own is drive to your office."

Claire blinked at the tone, a slight frown marring her forehead as she stared at Jackie.

"Oh now, you know I have to maintain some amount of independence, Jackie." He laughed as Claire pursed her lips, unsure if William was aware of the sudden tension in the room or if he didn't care. "Thanks again for bringing dinner." He pulled some money out of his pants pocket. "This should cover it."

Jackie broke contact with Claire and turned to William, smiling as she reached for the money.

"You're not staying for dinner?"

William answered for Jackie, shaking his head. "She never stays, always has things to do."

"You got that right, William." She walked out of the kitchen as Claire went to Eddie and picked him up. Jackie paused to look at the picture above the mantle.

"My great-grandfather."

"Nice picture." She continued toward the door with William escorting her but not before Claire caught her glancing at the trunk on the hearth.

***

After removing Eddie's bumblebee costume and settling him in his portable playpen, Claire sat on the sofa pulling one leg underneath her. "Dinner was delicious, William. Thank you."

William grunted as he slid the trunk off the hearth and dragged it to the sofa. "This beast is small but heavy. I had to have Ben, my foreman, carry it down from the attic. Whew." He sank down next to Claire and ran a trembling hand through his hair. "I enjoy having you and Jack here." William paused and stared at his snarled hands. "You two bring such joy to this old man."

Claire leaned over and hugged him. "We feel the same way." Curiosity got the better of her as she stared at the trunk. "Why don't you tell me about this exquisite antique trunk?"

The dome-topped trunk was fancier than she was expecting. The metal top had intricate carvings that continued down the front middle portion of the trunk. The rest of it was made of wood and was roughly three feet long by two-and-a-half feet high and sixteen inches deep. The handles were made of wood and the corners were reinforced with leather.

Claire ran her fingers over the side and along the cracks and knots in the wood before examining the carvings in the metal. "Wow! The intricacy of the carvings is beautiful. And it's in such good shape."

William cleared his throat. "It was actually Elizabeth's trunk. She brought it with her when she moved west to Texas. It's been passed down through the years."

"The detail and condition of it is remarkable. But William, how can that be? I was told that Billy Miner died in a shoot-out and never had kids."

"Maggie's been flapping her jaw, hasn't she? I love that old broad but she don't have a clue. Bah, no one believes me and that's just fine." He lovingly touched the trunk then raised his eyes to Claire, staring at her with an intensity she'd never seen before.

"As I told you before, he survived. One of his gang members who looked a lot like Billy and who was shot in his stomach convinced him to leave and he'd pretended to be Billy instead. His name was James and he was like a younger brother to Billy. He knew he wouldn't survive and wanted Billy to have a chance."

William glanced at the picture sitting on the mantle. "My great-grandfather was injured, shot in his back near his shoulder. He lived a quiet life with the woman who saved his life, a woman by the name of Elizabeth Swanson. As soon as he healed enough, he left to kill the one remaining gang member who betrayed them all and to move the treasure to one location."

Claire leaned forward, caught up in the story. "I read online that Ian Smalley gave up Billy and the gang to get medicine for his wife that the Rangers were withholding."

William nodded.

"If that was true and if Ian believed Billy was dead, why didn't he go to all the hiding places and take the treasure himself?"

"He was the last to join the gang and had only been to one location near Austin. The Rangers held their end of the bargain and gave Ian the medicine that he needed for his wife so he didn't immediately go get it because he had to care for her."

"So Billy was waiting for Ian?"

"Yep, he knew Ian would eventually want the treasure and would travel there, so he only had to wait for him to show up." William took a deep breath and opened the trunk.

The interior was lined with some sort of wallpaper, faded and yellowing, but still beautiful. There was no tray inside just a big open space. She inhaled through her nose. "My goodness. It smells old and musty. Divine." She inhaled again.

Reaching inside, William pulled out a Colt single action Army revolver. "This was his weapon of choice." He noticed her look of alarm. "No need to worry, my dear, there are no bullets in the gun. It hasn't been used in more than one hundred years."

Claire's eyes were round as saucers. "Look at the detail on it. It's beautiful!"

Setting the Colt on the sofa next to him, he reached in and pulled out a black cowboy hat, frayed and torn. "From what I've been told, this was Jimmy's hat. Whenever there was a heist, the gang wore the same outfits. They had to wear a black hat but each man selected his own. My great-grandfather's hat was unique whereas Jimmy's was plain. He had my great grandfather switch hats to help sell himself as Billy Miner to the Rangers."

"Wow!" Claire took a deep breath and let it out slowly. "There is so much to process here. So if Billy moved everything to one location, where is it?"

William shrugged. That's the three hundred million dollar question. I moved here in two thousand ten, a few years after my father died. I found a map almost twenty years ago and I've been looking for the treasure off and on since then."

Claire's jaw dropped. "Billy left a map?"

William nodded. "I found it in a secret compartment at the bottom of the trunk." He leaned over the trunk and shoved some items out of the way, exposing the bottom to Claire. Pulling a string in the back corner, he revealed a small compartment. It was empty. "The map is in a safe place, a place I'm sure Billy would appreciate." He chuckled. "I didn't want to risk leaving it in the trunk even though no one knows about it. I've studied the map for years, bought this property in case it matched one of the Xs on the map." He grinned in self-deprecation. "Not a sound reason to buy property, eh? I even believed the treasure could be here."

He shook his head. "Who knows if it's even in the Boerne area. If there is any treasure out there, I won't find it before I'm gone. I'm just an old fool and I'm too old to look for it anymore anyway."

"This is unbelievable."

Both were quiet as they studied the trunk.

"How did Billy die?"

William looked up from the trunk. "He was out hunting in eighteen-eighty-one and a black bear got him. My grandfather was two years old." He put the hat and revolver back inside the trunk and closed the lid.

"My goodness. Thank you for sharing your amazing history, William, I'm honored. It's fascinating and so much more interesting than my history."

William chuckled. "Oh go on."

Claire laughed. Hearing some soft snores coming from the playpen, she glanced at her watch. "I hate to say it, but I need to take my little one home and put him to bed."

They both stood. Claire walked over to the playpen and picked up Eddie who snuggled into her chest.

"Let me get your bag and Jack's costume." William picked up both items and they both walked to the front door.

"I'll get him strapped into his car seat and will come back for the playpen."

"Don't bother, my dear. I'm coming into town day after tomorrow and can bring it with me if that works for you."

Claire tapped her chin then nodded. "That works. Thanks."

William leaned down and kissed Eddie on his forehead before doing the same to Claire. "Thanks for listening to this old fool's stories. I'm always glad for the time we have together."

Claire kissed William on the cheek. "Me too. Have a good night and I'll see you soon."

"Count on it."

She walked to her car and was soon waving goodbye to William, who was standing on his porch.

Neither realized someone was only one hundred feet away, squatting next to a tree and watching them.

Chapter 5

After waving goodbye to Claire and Eddie, William closed the door. His shoulders drooped and he trudged to the living room, mumbling about his aching joints. Despite the crackling fire, he shivered. He shook his head, amazed at how different he was when Claire and Jack were in the house. They brought so much life to his day.

Stooping down, he picked up Jack's toys that were on the ground in front of the fireplace. "Don't you go eating these toys, Bear. They're not for you." He patted Bear's head as he dropped the stuffed puppy dog and two race cars into the playpen. Groaning, he rubbed his lower back. "I've got to stop doing that." His muttered words went unheeded by Bear who had gone back to sleep.

Hearing a rap on his kitchen door he recognized Ben and waved him inside, meeting him in the kitchen. Bear trotted over and scooted out the door after the obligatory pat from Ben.

"Howdy William. The cows from the north field arrived a couple hours ago and are in the pens now. We'll start branding them tomorrow."

"Excellent. Can I offer you some coffee?"

Ben shook his head. "Thanks but I need to wrap up a few things before I call it a night." He looked toward the fireplace and nodded toward the trunk. "Do you need me to carry that back up to the attic?"

"No, no. It can wait until tomorrow or the next day. Make sure you bring little Sarah by for some trick or treating before you go into town in the afternoon."

"Thanks William. She's a witch this year and she'll love showing off for you."

"How can an angel be a witch?"

Ben laughed. "Angel for you because she knows she'll get lots of goodies. You spoil her, William."

"Damn right I do." William slapped his knee. "In all seriousness, though, I appreciate everything you do for me, Ben, always have." He reached out his hand. Ben grasped it and the two shook. "You've been with me since the beginning. Sarah wasn't even born. Hell, you weren't even married back then. It's been a joy watching you find happiness."

Ben smiled. "I'm blessed for sure and I honestly can't imagine working anywhere else. Jill and I love living here. Sarah does as well." Ben took a deep breath. "If there's nothing else, I'll finish up and head on home."

"Of course. If I had a lovely wife and sweet daughter, I'd want to be home with them too."

Ben and William walked to the door that was still ajar.

"See you tomorrow afternoon."

William nodded. "Have a good evening Ben."

After closing the door, William made himself a decaf coffee then carried it to his bedroom down the hall, deciding to watch the news from there. His room was off the kitchen on the backside of the house. It was large but simplistic in terms of furniture and wall hangings, with a queen size bed against the far wall, one nightstand on the left side of the bed, and an oil painting of the lake on his property above it. Against the wall opposite the bed was a tall dresser with a small television sitting on top.

William set the coffee down on the nightstand and walked into the bathroom to prepare for bed. After situating himself on his bed, he leaned against the headboard and pulled the covers up to his waist. Clicking on the news, he relaxed and drank his coffee which was now tepid.

William jerked awake. Blinking a few times, he cocked his head to the side. The bedroom was dark, the only light coming from the crime show that was playing on television. He turned it off and sat up straighter to listen.

Scratching and whining finally met his ears. "Coming Bear." William sighed and swung his legs off the bed and to the floor. He rubbed his eyes then stood, swaying a little as dizziness hit him from standing up too fast. "Getting old ain't for sissies."

He walked out of the bedroom and into the kitchen. The lights were out in the kitchen and living room. Only the light of the dying fire lit the room.

William frowned. How odd. He didn't remember turning them off.

That was his last thought before the bullet struck him between the eyes. He fell to the ground and a pool of blood gathered beneath his head.

Bear was still barking and whining outside the kitchen door. The intruder walked over to the door and opened it. Bear raced in and skidded to a stop, looking from the person at the door to William on the ground. Growling, he low-crawled over to William never taking his eyes off the intruder, who had closed the door. When Bear reached William, the growls turned into whining. He laid down next to him and put his head on William's stomach.

The intruder watched Bear for a moment before walking into the living room, picking up the trunk, and stepping outside. Pausing at the top step on the porch, the intruder looked to the left before rushing down the stairs and disappearing into the night.

Chapter 6

"Thanks so much for inviting us along and for picking us up." Claire hugged Grace and Ethan. Ethan picked up Jack's car seat and walked to the other side where he opened the passenger door and installed it behind the driver's seat.

"We're so glad you could join us," replied Grace. "And we just had to see this cute little bumblebee." She tickled Eddie's tummy as Claire held him which sent him into a fit of giggles. "Jo actually suggested we all go trick-or-treating since we have Ginger and Louise for the night."

Claire poked her head into the van. "Hi girls!" She walked to the other side and handed Eddie to Ethan as a chorus of hello's assailed her, then returned to Grace's side.

As soon as Eddie saw Jo, his eyes lit up and he chanted "Jo, Jo, Jo…" while bouncing up and down in Ethan's arms.

"Hold on there, buddy." Ethan got Eddie settled, and kissed him on the top of his head before closing the door.

Claire looked at Grace, a question in her eyes.

Grace leaned in close to Claire's ear. "Kent got a last-minute call…a murder, so we said we'd take the girls. Only Ginger plans to trick or treat. Jo and Louise say they're too old." She rolled her eyes, chuckling. "Teens."

Ginger and Louise were Kent's daughters. Ginger, twelve years old, was at that age between childhood and adulthood, wanting to do things children do but also enjoying dressing up when the occasion warranted. Louise, on the other hand, was fourteen going on twenty-five.

Claire laughed and settled herself behind Grace then looked at Ethan as he pulled away from the curb. Ethan Marshall was tall, good-looking, and all cowboy. "I have to say, Ethan, that your cowboy image is taking a hit driving this van not to mention watching rom-coms." She grinned.

His hazel eyes shot to hers through the rearview mirror. "Hey, you'd better be careful or I might have to arrest you for cowboy harassment."

"Cowboy harassment? That's a new one, detective!" Grace playfully punched him in his arm as the adults laughed.

Claire leaned forward and squeezed Ethan's shoulder. "Congratulations, Ethan!"

"Thanks. We're pretty excited." He winked at Grace.

Ethan drove them to the Esperanza subdivision, a short drive from downtown. "A buddy of mine lives at Esperanza. There are lots of homes and lots of families, plenty of opportunities to trick-or-treat." He wiggled his eyes up and down as the girls cheered. "Hey, I thought only Ginger was trick-or-treating tonight."

Jo stuck her tongue out at Ethan. "I'm going to help Eddie so naturally I'll get some of the candy."

"And I'm helping my little sister. She'll share with me." Louise giggled as she hugged Ginger.

"Don't count on it." Ginger playfully pushed her away.

The good-natured ribbing continued until Ethan parked in front of a modest two-story home. Ethan got out of the van and walked up the driveway, shaking hands with a balding man as everyone climbed out of the car.

As soon as his feet hit the sidewalk, Eddie raced over to Jo. She laughed and picked him up, squeezing him in a tight hug. Claire smiled. They had become buddies, and she recognized that he missed seeing Jo.

She took a moment to check out the neighborhood. It was clean with sidewalks on both sides of the street. All the houses had manicured yards and continued as far as she could see.

Even at six-thirty, with sunset only twenty minutes away it was still hot and muggy. Claire was grateful to be wearing a sleeveless summer dress with her sandals.

The sidewalk and street were already teeming with kids in their costumes making the rounds with animated chatter. Claire was warm in her dress and imagined that the clowns, witches, storm troopers, and others were baking inside their costumes.

Jo took Eddie's hand and followed Ginger and Louise down the sidewalk with the adults following. Claire took countless pictures and some video of Eddie as he went up to each house.

The decorations in the neighborhood were festive, colorful, and at times spooky. They passed a few houses with oversized spiders and webs in the bushes, skeletons hanging from trees, and scary music playing. Eddie wouldn't go up to the doors of those houses. Other homes had blow-up Sponge Bobs or other characters. And some had colorful lights strung up in the trees.

Claire sniffed appreciatively and groaned. "That is just cruel to pop popcorn where everyone can smell it." Ginger and Louise had already run over to the house across the street where it was being made. Jo and Eddie were not far behind.

"I'm going to have to pop some tonight just so Ethan can enjoy it." Grace laughed then shook her head when Ethan jogged over to get in line with the girls. "Well, I'll have to make more popcorn. That little bag will not satisfy him for long." She gave a thumbs up to Ethan when he held up a bag with a big grin on his face.

Claire laughed as she and Grace crossed the street to join the others.

By the time they returned to the car, Claire was carrying a sleepy boy and the girls were gabbing about the cute boys. The chatter inside the car was much more subdued on the return trip. When Ethan pulled up at her office, she said goodbye to Grace and the girls then Ethan helped her with the car seat since she was carrying a sleeping Jack. They said their goodbyes after he set the car seat in the office foyer.

Claire locked the office door, walked to the back, and carried Eddie up to their apartment. It was much later than his usual bedtime so he didn't fuss at all when she changed his diaper, put his dinosaur pajamas on, and laid him in his bed. Kissing his forehead, she walked out of the bedroom, closing the door behind her. A bath could wait until tomorrow.

She'd just poured herself a glass of wine when there was a knock on her door. Not expecting anyone, she walked over to the window by her dining table and peeked outside the curtain. She dropped the curtain and stepped back, her mouth hanging open.

Kent. She hadn't seen him in a couple of months. Her heartbeat increased and her palms began to sweat. *Damn it! How can he possibly look sexier, even in uniform, well maybe because of the uniform? Stop, I don't care about him anymore, I never cared about him.*

She waited until her breathing returned to normal before opening the door.

Kent's arm was raised to knock again. He dropped it and they stood looking at each other in silence for what seemed like an eternity.

"Are you Claire St. John?"

Startled, Claire looked to her right and realized a man in uniform stood next to Kent. She hadn't noticed him. He was shorter than Kent and stocky, some might say he was overweight. With thinning salt-and-pepper hair and narrow dark eyes, he didn't look like a pleasant man and he was currently scowling at her.

Claire was a little taken aback. "Yes I am. Who are you?"

"Claire, this is Deputy Hanson."

"What's going on Kent?"

"Ma'am…"

"I'll take it from here Jeremy." Kent shot his partner a warning look. "Can we come in?"

She studied Kent. "I just put Eddie down. I don't want him to wake up."

"We'll be quiet and we won't be long."

Claire opened the door wider and both men stepped inside. Shutting the door behind them, she turned to

Kent. "This is obviously some sort of official business so I'll ask again…what's going on?"

"William Miner was murdered."

Chapter 7

TEARS WELLED IN CLAIRE'S EYES AND rolled down her cheeks. Taking two shaky steps back, she bumped into the door and her knees buckled. "Whaaat?"

"Claire!" Kent caught her around the waist before she fell and helped her to a stool at the kitchen counter. Walking to the pantry, he grabbed a napkin and returned, handing it to her.

"Oh God." She wiped her eyes and face then blew her nose. Placing her elbow on the counter, she cupped her chin in her hand, sniffling and taking shaky breaths. She looked up at Kent. "Murdered? How? When?"

"Sometime last night. We got the call this afternoon and arrived at his house a little after six. His foreman found William when he brought his daughter to the house to show him her costume. He said he spoke with William at eight last night but didn't see him all day. The JP pronounced him this afternoon but has ordered an autopsy to pinpoint the exact time."

Boerne and Kendall County have no coroners, so the Justice of the Peace is called to murder scenes. The JP not only pronounces time of death but he is also the only one who determines if an autopsy is warranted and who can order it.

Deputy Hanson stepped toward them. "We understand you were with him last night."

Claire frowned, her eyes moving from Kent to Deputy Hanson. "Yes, Eddie and I had dinner with him. William must have spoken with Ben right after we left."

"You normally have dinner with him on Sundays, right?"

Claire's eyes shot back to Kent as she stood. She peered at him, lips thinning. "That's right. I took Eddie to the church on Sunday afternoon for a Halloween event. William and I changed our dinner to Wednesday." She paused. "Why isn't Ethan with you?"

"William lived outside of Boerne so this case fell to the county." Kent was the Lieutenant in Charge of the Criminal Investigation Division for the county, had been for over a year. "Deputy Hanson will be working on this with me."

"You're a single mom, right?" Deputy Hanson's eyes scanned the room. "And you own your own business? Must be hard to do it all on your own. Having a friend, especially a wealthy friend like William, must be nice."

Claire gasped.

Kent took a step toward his partner. "Deputy Hanson…"

Jeremy held up his hands in a placating gesture. "I'm just trying to understand the relationship between Ms. St. John and the deceased."

"William was a dear friend and I don't like the tone or the insinuation, Deputy." Her eyes flashed as she glared at him.

"I'm not insinuating anything, just trying to gather facts, ma'am."

Claire walked past them and yanked open the door. "We're done here. You need to leave."

Deputy Hanson sauntered up to her. "We'll need you to come into the office to give a more detailed statement." He tipped his hat as he walked past her. "Ma'am."

Kent walked over to her. "Claire…"

"Good night, Lieutenant."

Kent held her stare before sighing and rubbing the back of his neck. "Don't drive to the office. We'll come back."

"You're welcome to stop by my office during office hours. Don't come to my home again."

He paused before breaking eye contact. "Good night Claire." He walked out the door.

Locking the door, Claire slid to the floor and let the tears flow.

Chapter 8

"WHAT THE HELL WAS THAT ALL about Jeremy?" Kent stepped in front of him to halt his progress to the car.

"I was doing our job, Lieutenant."

"Bullshit. Since when do you accuse someone with no provocation or cause?" He glared at Jeremy.

Deputy Hanson held his stare, his lip curled up in a smirk. "Your judgement is skewed where Ms. St. John is concerned, Lieutenant." He sidestepped Kent and continued to the car. "We should have continued the interrogation."

Kent was an affable guy. He was good at his job and usually got along with people, especially those with whom he worked. He and Ethan had worked seamlessly together on multiple cases over the years. It helped that they were best friends growing up, of course, and Kent lived on the ranch next to his. But they respected and complemented each other, both comfortable in their positions and areas of expertise.

Jeremy Hanson was a different story, though. He had worked at the sheriff's department for about twenty-five years now. When Kent had joined the force right out of college as a deputy, Jeremy was already a senior deputy. Back then, he was helpful and showed Kent how things were done. But as Kent moved up and eventually surpassed Jeremy when he was promoted to lieutenant last year, Jeremy had become more distant, clearly resentful, and his bitterness had on more than one occasion spilled over into work. Like now.

Jeremy had recently moved to the Criminal Investigation Division and Kent was his superior. This was Jeremy's second case as an investigator, his first murder, and their first case working together. His first case had been a relatively simple burglary. Kent's hope that they could work seamlessly together was fading fast. He settled himself into the driver's seat then turned to face Jeremy.

"Be careful, Deputy Hanson. Your tone with Claire St. John and certainly with me is not acceptable and will cease right now. In addition, you will speak to no one related to this case without my permission or unless I'm with you. Is that clear?" His blue eyes were like steel as they held Jeremy's eyes.

The tension was palpable as Jeremy stared at Kent but after a few tense seconds, his shoulders rolled in and he seemed to deflate. He broke eye contact and turned his head to stare out the window. "Crystal."

Kent let out a breath he didn't realize he was holding. "Good. We have a lot of work ahead of us. Ben Capshaw, William's foreman, also said that Jackie Baker was at the house yesterday so we'll need to talk to her and I want to go back to the house to ask Capshaw a few more questions. We'll talk to St. John again but first up is the autopsy. I was informed by the Holt & Holt Funeral Home that William's body will be transported to a mortuary in San

Antonio for the autopsy tomorrow morning. We're going to go with the body and observe the autopsy."

"You're kidding! Why not just wait for the report?" Jeremy groused.

Kent glanced at him and frowned before shifting his eyes back to the road.. "They're notoriously backed up and it could easily be ten to twelve weeks before we get official results. You know this, Jeremy." Boerne did not have the facilities to perform autopsies. Bodies were transported either to Austin or San Antonio. Law officers were allowed to observe autopsies from a separate room and take notes, however they could not interact with the medical examiner. "The body is being transported at nine am so we need to be at the funeral home at eight-forty-five."

Jeremy muttered something under his breath

Kent now understood why Jeremy hadn't been promoted. Taking shortcuts and sitting back and waiting was not something Kent was willing to do. He pulled into the station next to Jeremy's car and turned his head, staring at Jeremy. "We leave from here tomorrow morning at eight-thirty sharp."

Jeremy gave a quick nod and got out of the vehicle. Kent pulled out of the parking lot and headed home. His thoughts turned to William. Who would kill such a nice old man? And why?

***

November 2024

News of William's murder was the talk of the town. No one could understand why anyone would want him dead, even if many deemed him a little loco for always talking as if he was related to Billy Miner simply because they had the same name.

The next morning, Claire was sitting at her desk in the office when her phone rang. She wasn't in the right frame of mind to talk to any clients, and almost let it go to voicemail, since she couldn't concentrate. Recognizing that she had a business to run and had to keep going, she answered the call.

"Good morning. Claire St. John."

"Good morning, Ms. St. John. My name is Clarence Booker of Booker Law Offices. I'm calling regarding William Miner."

Just the mention of his name was enough to bring tears to her eyes. She cleared her throat and pinched the bridge of her nose. "How can I help you Mr. Booker?"

"William established a will a couple of months ago as well as a living trust. He named you as the executor."

"Me?" Claire croaked out. "I don't…I'm not…" She took a shaky breath.

"I understand this is a difficult time, and I'm sorry for your loss. William was a good friend of mine as well and I still can't believe he's gone."

"Thank you, Mr. Booker."

"Clarence, please."

"Clarence. And call me Claire." Having gone through the process when Michael died, Claire understood the ramifications of what Clarence was telling her. "He told me about the will and trust just last week. I had been hammering him for quite some time about setting one up for obvious reasons."

"The trust was a last-minute decision as we were drawing up his will. Most of his holdings are in the trust so there won't be much that will be held in probate. As the executor for William, we'll need to meet to go over everything and outline your duties."

"This is all a bit overwhelming."

"I'm sure it is but you don't need to worry. I'll be with you every step of the way. Now when can we meet? My preference is this afternoon, if at all possible. We have a lot to go over."

After settling on a time, Claire brought up a funeral for William.

"Ah yes. It looks like the medical examiner in San Antonio will release William's body on Thursday. William was very fond of you and he requested in his will that you handle the arrangements. I have some details that we can discuss this afternoon. He wanted something simple. If you can't do that…"

Claire sniffed. "Of course I'll make the arrangements for him."

"Excellent. I'll see you this afternoon then. Thank you Claire."

Claire hung up the phone and placed her elbows on the desk. Resting her face in her hands and closing her eyes she inhaled deeply and exhaled slowly. She wasn't sure how long she stayed like this, but she raised her head when the bell at the front office door jingled.

There was a knock on the door and it slowly opened. "Claire, it's Grace." She poked her head inside. "I hope I'm not interrupting."

"A most welcome interruption, Grace. Come in." Claire stood and walked over to her.

Grace hugged her. "Ethan told me about William this morning and it was all over the local news. How are you doing?"

"I'm still in a state of shock." She motioned for Grace to have a seat, then settled back into her chair behind the desk. "I haven't been able to get anything done today. I rescheduled all appointments I had and will no doubt need to reschedule more next week." She paused. "I just found out that William made me the executor of his will."

She took a sip of water. "I had been hounding him for weeks to get his will done. Everyone should have a will, right?" She shook her head as she looked at Grace. "He finally did it." Claire rubbed her temple. "I'm meeting with the lawyer later today. Not only that, I'm planning his funeral which will most likely be next weekend."

"Wow!" Grace leaned back in her seat. "That's a lot to take on. All of this speaks of how much William loved you. I'm glad he had you in his life, Claire, and I'll help any way you need it."

Claire sighed. "William was the sweetest man. Who could possibly have done this?" Grabbing a tissue, she dabbed her eyes and blew her nose.

"Oh hon! I know how close you and Eddie were to him." She looked around the office. "Speaking of... where's that cutie pie today?"

"He's at daycare. I'll pick him up at... Oh shoot. I'm meeting with the lawyer at two and I'm supposed to pick him up at two-thirty."

"I'll pick him up and take him to the ranch. He loves the animals and Jo will enjoy playing with him when she gets home from volleyball practice."

"Grace, I don't want to impose..."

Grace reached across the desk and patted Claire's hand. "I meant what I said about helping you. Let me do this. In fact, you're coming over for dinner tonight. No excuses. Whenever you get done with the lawyer, drive over."

Claire sagged a little in relief. "That would be wonderful. Thanks so much, Grace. I appreciate it."

Chapter 9

CLAIRE HAD BEEN TO ETHAN'S RANCH once or twice but today was the first time the hydrangeas lining the path to the front entrance were in full bloom. The blues, pinks, and whites of the tiny flowers entranced her.

"Knock, knock," she called out as she opened the door.

"Come on in Claire," Grace chimed from the kitchen. Claire walked through the living room and into the kitchen. Grace was draining hot water from a pot. "I'm so glad you're here. Help yourself to some wine." She nodded toward an open bottle of wine sitting on the counter.

"Hmmmm…pinot noir, my favorite. Can I help with anything?"

Grace placed the pot of noodles back on the stove and added a cheese sauce. "Yes. You can sit down and keep me company while I finish making this mac-n-cheese for the kids. Jo and Chase took Eddie to the barn and Ethan is out back barbecuing." She gasped and stopped what she was doing. Turning her gaze to Claire, she grimaced. "I've got to say this real fast before they arrive. Ethan had already invited Kent and the girls to dinner. They should be here any minute. I'm so sorry."

Claire inhaled through her nose then exhaled. "You don't have to apologize. We live in a small town and we've run into each other already a few times. I'll enjoy seeing Ginger and Louise again, twice in one week."

Grace turned back to the stove as the back door opened and Ethan walked inside carrying a platter of meat.

At the same time, the front door opened and Louise and Ginger raced inside, followed more slowly by Kent.

Everyone was talking at once.

"Claire!" Ginger wrapped her arms around Claire's waist and squeezed.

Laughing, Claire squeezed back and kissed the top of her head. "I saw you just two days ago kiddo."

Ginger leaned back and in a dramatic tone exclaimed, "That was AGES ago."

Claire looked over Ginger. "Hi Louise! Did Ginger share any of her candy with you?"

"She only gave me two tootsie-rolls and three lollipops." She scrunched her nose and playfully shoved her sister out of the way, giving Claire a quick hug before walking into the kitchen to hug Grace.

Ethan glanced at Kent as he placed the meat on the counter. "Good timing old man. I just brought the meat inside."

Kent shook his head, grinning. "Watch who you're calling an old man, you geezer." His smile slipped when he reached Claire. "Hi Claire."

"Louise, give Jo and Chase a call. Dinner is ready."

"Hon, I already gave them a shout. They're on their way in." Ethan leaned in and kissed Grace before washing his hands at the sink.

Claire just stared into Kent's blue eyes, unable to move or speak. Despite how the evening ended last night, he still had the power to make her forget where she was.

The back door opened.

"Mama, Mama, Mama." Eddie wriggled out of Jo's arms and ran to Claire.

Claire blinked twice, and her cheeks turned a delicate pink. Frowning when she witnessed the corners of Kent's mouth twitching upward, she focused on Eddie racing over to her as fast as his legs could carry him. Laughing, she picked him up. "How's my sweet boy?" She lifted him high and kissed his belly, making loud smacking noises.

He giggled and leaned down, giving her a slobbery kiss on her head. When he looked up, a smile split his face. "Da, Da, Da." Eddie tried calling Kent 'Dad' when they were dating, but couldn't quite get that second 'd' out of his mouth. He reached for Kent with both arms.

Claire handed Eddie to Kent and turned away before he saw the regret in her eyes. Try as she might, she couldn't remember why she ended their budding relationship.

"Dinner everyone. Belly up to the bar." Grace had laid out the salad, steaks, French bread, macaroni and cheese, and green beans on the kitchen island. "There's plenty here, so help yourself. Jo, why don't you, Chase, Louise, and Ginger eat at the table on the back patio. It's not too hot out there."

As the kids filled their plates, Claire excused herself and went into one of the bedrooms to change Eddie. By the time she returned, the adults were serving themselves.

Kent placed his dinner plate on the table and walked back to Claire who was approaching the kitchen island with her son in her arms.

"Let me take him while you get a plate for yourself and some for him."

"Oh…um, thanks." She handed Eddie to Kent.

As soon as she sat down, he handed Eddie back to her. Talk was lively as the four adults ate, Claire alternating between giving herself a couple of bites to Eddie's one. He happily gurgled and played with Claire's hair in between bites.

Jo and Chase came inside to get some cookies for the four teens. As Chase grabbed a plate and piled cookies on it, Jo walked over to Claire.

"Let me take him so you can finish your meal, Claire."

"Thanks, Jo, I appreciate it."

Jo reached down and picked up Eddie. "Are you kidding? Any time I can spend with him is a treat for me." Smiling, she joined Chase and they walked out the door.

When dinner was finished, Grace and Claire cleared the table while Ethan and Kent walked over to the living room and settled themselves on the sofa. Claire brought a plate of cookies to the living room and set them on the coffee table while Grace came in shortly thereafter carrying a tray with four mugs of coffee, a small pitcher of cream, and assorted sugars. She sat down on the matching sofa across from her husband and next to Claire.

Picking up a mug, Grace leaned back and half-turned to her right, tucking her leg underneath her so she could face Claire. "How did it go with the lawyer today?" She blew on her coffee.

Kent had just picked up his mug. "Lawyer?" He took a sip, staring at Claire over the rim.

Not aware of what had transpired between Kent and Claire the night before, Grace continued. "Claire was named executor of William's will. That's why we had Eddie this afternoon. She was meeting with him. Claire is also organizing his funeral, all at William's request of course."

"Is that so? When did all of this happen?"

Claire shifted in her seat, suddenly uncomfortable and feeling as if she was about to be interrogated. Her narrowed eyes shot to Kent's and she sat up a little straighter. "I found out this morning when his lawyer called me."

"I'm so glad William listened to you, Claire." At the question she read in Ethan and Kent's eyes, Grace added, "He only finished his will a few months ago, right Claire? And that was only after Claire convinced him to set it up."

"So you told him to get a will and now you're the executor?"

Claire's lips formed a thin line at the veiled insinuation. "Kent, as his financial advisor, of course I told him it would be a good idea to have a will. I had no idea he would make me the executor."

Sensing the sudden tension in the room, Ethan frowned at Kent speaking for the first time. "Claire, you gave William sound advice. No one could have known that his will would come into play so soon."

Claire looked away from Kent, making an effort to relax. "Thank you Ethan. I'm still in shock. William was a wonderful man, Eddie loved him like a grandfather. I miss him so much."

"Every time I spoke with him he was smiling and was very nice." Grace shook her head. "You said the funeral will be this coming weekend?"

Claire nodded. "Yes. Mr. Booker said it looks like they'll release William's body on Thursday so I'm planning on a celebration of life at his ranch on Saturday. I spoke with Ben Capshaw as I was driving here and he's going to help. William wanted something simple, no fanfare."

"And the reading of the will?" Kent's question hung in the air.

Claire's eyes shifted to him. "Mr. Booker will notify those who are in the will this week and the reading will occur after the celebration of life." Her eyes narrowed, fuming at his repeated insinuations. It was time to go.

Setting her mug down, she looked at Grace as she stood up. "I'm sorry to do this but I have to get Eddie home. I'll go grab him now." Without waiting for a response, she walked to the back door and stepped outside.

When she returned with Eddie, Ethan and Grace were waiting for her near the back door.

"Thank you both for dinner tonight and for looking after this squirt." She hugged Ethan. "The steaks were perfect."

"Glad you could come, Claire. You two are always welcome." He tousled Eddie's hair.

She hugged Grace who whispered, "What the heck is going on?"

"We'll talk later, Grace. I'm so sorry to be leaving like this."

Grace shook her head. "No need to apologize. I'll call you."

Claire turned toward the living room. Kent was standing by the sofa holding Eddie's bag.

"I'll walk you out."

Seeing the look on his face, she scowled but said nothing, just turned toward the door.

Fussing, Eddie used his hands to push on Claire's arms. "Mama, no."

Claire looked down at Eddie. His crocodile tears were nearly her undoing. "I'm sorry, honey. Was Mama holding you too tight?" She loosened her grip, kissed him on his forehead, and tickled his chin. Her tactics worked. Eddie threw back his head, giggling.

Kent opened the front door and both walked outside to her car. Neither said a word as he placed the bag in the front passenger seat while Claire settled Eddie in his car seat in the back.

"Claire…"

She turned to him, hands fisted at her sides, the open passenger door between them. "Is that how it's going to be from now on, Kent, every time we see each other I get interrogated?" She glared at him. "I do not appreciate your repeated insinuations."

"I wasn't…"

"The hell you weren't." She was breathing hard.

"Look at it from my perspective…"

"Which one? I thought I was with a friend tonight not the lieutenant." Her anger fell away and her eyes filled with tears. "William was my friend. More than that, he was like a father to me. You know that."

Kent sighed. Placing both hands on top of the car door, he stared into her eyes. "I am your friend, Claire. But I'm also an officer of the law. If I sounded like I was accusing you of anything, I apologize. I know you didn't kill William. You loved him and it was clear that he adored you." He looked up at the stars and took a deep breath before releasing it and looking back at her. "But I have a responsibility to fully investigate his murder and that means I have to ask some uncomfortable questions at times."

Claire angrily brushed the tears from her cheeks. "I get that. But it would be nice if you asked those questions at an appropriate time, not when we're dining with friends."

Kent nodded. "You're right and I apologize." He reached for a loose tendril of her hair and lifted it. "The auburn highlights suit you." He tucked her hair behind her ear. "Am I forgiven?"

Claire sniffed, managing a watery smile. "Stop looking at me with those puppy dog eyes." She stepped back and closed the passenger door signaling the end of the conversation. "Thank you for your help with Eddie." She walked past him to the driver's side of the car and opened the car door.

"Claire…"

Claire paused and looked at Kent over the car.

"One more official thing. Deputy Hanson and I will need to be present at the reading of the will."

"I'll have Mr. Booker get in touch with you. Good night Kent."

Chapter 10

WILLIAM'S CELEBRATION OF LIFE WAS HELD at one o'clock in the afternoon on what was turning out to be a hot and sunny November day. Clarence had given her a budget, an amount stipulated by William, for his service. Claire had used some of her own money to supplement what Clarence gave her because William deserved it.

She lined the path leading from the driveway around the house with pots that were filled with yellow and orange chrysanthemums. In the back, a large white tent had been set up. It was open on all sides but Claire, with Ben's help, had created an entrance using the pots of flowers. A rectangular table with a white tablecloth was set up just inside the tent entrance with a guest registry for people to sign and pictures of William at various stages of his life that Claire had found, as well as some she'd taken with William and Eddie.

At the far end of the tent was a bar with sodas, water, sweet tea, and a variety of beers for folks to enjoy. The ranch hands staffed it. Three rectangular tables with white tablecloths were on the back side and would soon be filled with ribs, sausage, brisket, beans, rice guacamole and tortillas. Tables and chairs filled the center.

Ben, his wife Jill, and Claire greeted the guests as they arrived. Their daughter, Sarah, played with Eddie in an enclosed shaded area on the grass next to the tent. Fifty people had been invited and it looked like everyone was going to be there. Claire nodded at Kent and Deputy Hanson when they arrived.

"Claire, it looks amazing." Grace gave Claire a hug when she arrived with Ethan, Chase, Jo, and Jo's boyfriend.

Claire smiled. "Thanks Grace. It's probably a little more than the simple William asked for, but I wanted him to go out in style."

"I think it's perfect."

"Go on inside and grab a seat. We'll start soon."

Jo hugged Claire. "Hi Claire, this is my boyfriend Sam. Do you mind if I take Eddie to our table?"

"It's nice to meet you Sam. Of course I don't mind. Thank you so much. Would you mind also taking Sarah, if that's all right with Jill?"

"Absolutely."

At Jill's nod, Jo and Sam went over to get Sarah and Eddie, then they joined Ethan and Grace at a table they had selected.

"Hi Claire."

Claire turned her head. "Jackie! I'm so glad you could make it."

"I don't understand how anyone could hurt him." She sniffed. "I really miss him and still pick up the phone to call him…"

Claire hugged her. "I miss him too. The police are doing their job and I hope they find his killer soon, but today is a day to celebrate the incredible life William had. You know Ben and Jill, right?"

Jackie said hello to Ben and barely acknowledged Jill before nodding at Claire and heading inside. *What's up with that?* Claire didn't have time to ponder that as more guests approached them.

When most people had arrived, Ben, Jill, and Claire went inside to mingle. Spying Maggie with her son, Claire wove between tables chatting with folks until she reached them.

"Maggie, thank you for being here and thank you both for catering the meal today."

Maggie hooted. "Well, no need to thank us. You're paying after all."

"Mother." Dale shook his head.

Claire chuckled. "Maggie…" Still smiling, she turned to Dale. "If I don't get a chance, be sure to thank your son for preparing the food. It's not your typical bistro fare but William loved a good Texas barbecue."

"It's our pleasure and just because we don't serve it in the bistro doesn't mean we don't enjoy eating it. We are Texans after all." Dale smiled.

After thanking them again, Grace wove through the tables making her way back to the table at the entrance where a microphone had been stashed.

Turning it on, she tapped it a couple of times.

"Good afternoon everyone. Can y'all hear me? Thank you for coming to William's celebration of life today. And this is indeed a celebration." Claire paused and acknowledged every person at every table before continuing. "William had a long and amazing life and all of us were lucky enough to share in part of it." More nods from the guests. "William didn't want a typical funeral. He didn't want anything special, just a simple service. To me, that speaks to the kind of man he was…humble and caring, crotchety at times."

Claire chuckled with others in the crowd. "He was someone who may have been a loner to most, but to those he loved he was always there for them. I know this first-hand…" Claire paused, swallowing a few times. Ben, who was standing next to her, handed her a bottle of water. Nodding her thanks, she took a few sips. "William was one of the first people I met when I arrived in Boerne. He was kind and funny. Eddie immediately took to him. And boy did William love Eddie. He came to the office regularly, ostensibly to talk finances, but more often than not he just wanted to hang out. And if he came on a day that Eddie was in the office with me, well it made his day."

Claire smiled at the memory and perused the room. "So many of us have special memories of William. This is a celebration so I want to open this up to others who might like to share memories they have." She looked at Ben. "Ben, would you like to be the first?"

Ben nodded and took the microphone. He spoke of his friendship for twenty minutes, before passing the microphone to someone else. All in all, eight people spoke about William and shared their stories.

At last, the microphone was returned to Claire. "Wow! Thank you to all who shared your memories. I'm so moved by your beautiful stories." She looked around the room. "Well without further ado, let's eat." The kids cheered, making the adults laugh.

Claire laughed as well. "All right. If you hold on for just a few minutes, the food is going to be brought out and we'll get things going. Oh, and I want to thank Barkley's Bistro for catering the delicious meal we're going to have. It's not their normal fare. Today, we're having a Texas barbecue with all the fixin's. Thanks again for coming and enjoy the lunch."

The afternoon was filled with plenty of laughter as folks shared stories about William.

"You did good, Claire. This was an amazing send-off for William." Grace walked over to Claire, who was bouncing Eddie on her hip.

"Aww, thanks. It looks like everyone is enjoying themselves, which is exactly what William would have liked."

"We're going to head home. Ethan has a sick horse he's been keeping an eye on."

"Thanks again, Grace, for coming today. I appreciate it. Tell Ethan that I hope his horse is okay."

Other guests slowly departed, paying final respects to Claire and Ben as they made their way to their cars.

Clarence Booker, who was also present for the celebration, walked up to Claire. "All beneficiaries are here, of course, so we'll begin at three-thirty as originally planned."

Claire nodded. "The rest of the guests should be gone in the next five or ten minutes. Let's meet in the living room."

"I'll let everyone know."

"Thank you, Clarence." Claire watched him walk away and wiped her free hand on the side of her dress. It was time to read the will.

Chapter 11

CLAIRE WAS THE LAST TO ARRIVE in the living room. Clarence had pulled a chair over from the dining room and was seated near the hearth with his back to the fireplace. Situated on his left on one sofa were Jackie and Maggie. Ben was sitting on the opposite sofa and there was an unoccupied seat next to him for Claire. Standing near the window by the front door was Deputy Hanson, feet planted shoulder width apart and arms crossed. And leaning against the back wall was Kent.

"Would anyone like anything to drink before I sit down?" Claire made eye contact with everyone, continuing to her seat next to Ben when all shook their heads.

Clarence cleared his throat. "Excellent, then we can begin. My name is Clarence Booker and I was William's lawyer." He scratched his head. "Actually before I proceed, I want to thank Claire for making all the arrangements for William's celebration of life. She followed William's wishes and I'm sure he would have been pleased."

Claire blushed under his praise but nodded her thanks. "Ben was a huge help. I couldn't have done it without him."

"Of course, thank you Ben." Clarence reached into his pocket and pulled out a pair of glasses. "Well, let's get down to business." He reached for his briefcase and placed it on his lap. Opening it, he pulled a document out and closed the lid. Using his briefcase as a table, he set the document on it and lifted his head to look at everyone. "A few months ago, William came to my office and wanted to set up a will. We talked about the will as well as a trust, to avoid probate, and he did both. We finished both fairly quickly because he knew what he wanted and kept things simple. You may or may not be aware that Claire is the executor of the will. She has not yet seen it and has asked that I read it, preferring to hear it at the same time as all of you. As executor, though, she will be responsible for ensuring that you receive your item or items."

Sensing everyone's eyes on her, Claire forced herself to sit quietly with her hands folded in her lap.

Clarence cleared his throat again before proceeding. The first part of the will was the standard boring but necessary legal-ease verbiage that was included in all wills.

He stopped at the top of page three. "Enough of all the legal stuff. I'm sure you want to get to all the good stuff so here we go. Oh, legally you are entitled to a copy of this will. My office will mail a copy to each of you via certified mail so look for it in the coming days." He took a deep breath. "All of the following is in William's own words." He cleared his throat.

"To Margaret Anderson, you've been a good friend from the time I arrived in this sleepy town. We're two old codgers and there ain't much you don't already have or could buy if you wanted. But you always admired my fifty-seven Chevy so I want you to have it. The blue color will go nicely with your eyes."

Claire glanced at Maggie who was shaking her head and dabbing her eyes.

"That old goat…flirtin' even in death."

Everyone chuckled, bringing a smile from Maggie.

"To Jackie Baker…"

Jackie leaned forward.

"You are such a hard worker whether assisting the principal at the school, helping me, even helping Claire with Jack. Don't think it went unnoticed. The time you took to bring me dinners and buy groceries, not to mention the countless other errands you ran for me, was so appreciated. I count myself lucky that day we met in HEB in twenty-twenty-three. I'm giving you twenty-five thousand dollars. You once told me you wanted to take a nice vacation to Europe one day and I hope this will get you there in style."

Claire cocked her head, perplexed. There was a spark of anger in Jackie's eyes. While she schooled her features quickly, her clenched hands and white knuckles told a different story.

"That is…generous of William," she replied stiffly. "I guess I'm going to Europe next summer." The barest hint of warmth touched her expression.

Clarence continued. "Ben, you have been the glue that has kept this ranch going. More than that, you've been a good friend to this old fool. I appreciate you and have enjoyed our talks. Thank you for all that you did for me. The house you, Jill and Sarah share is yours with rights to the driveway to access the main street for as long as you want it. If you choose to sell at a future date, it has to go back to the ranch. You'll get a fair price, of course. But I hope you'll stay. The foreman job is yours for as long as you want it with a guaranteed ten percent raise every two years. In addition, an education fund in the amount of eighty-thousand dollars will be established for Sarah's college education."

"Wow!" Ben was shaking his head. "I never expected that kind of generosity. And for him to provide for Sarah's college? Jill will be in tears over this. Hell, I'm in tears over this." He sniffed,

Claire leaned toward Ben and squeezed his shoulder. A movement caught her eye and she glanced toward the front door. Deputy Hanson stared at her with narrowed eyes. A little nonplussed, her eyes shifted to Kent. He was no longer leaning against the wall but was standing in a similar position as Deputy Hanson, feet braced apart and arms folded across his chest. He was watching everyone with a keen eye, not missing anything.

"For Clyde and Erwin, the two ranch hands who work here. I have appreciated their loyalty and hard work through the years. They both have been here over ten years. They're family. They have a job here as long as they want it and will each receive ten thousand dollars. Their pay increases will be determined by Claire and Ben on a timeframe they establish." Clarence pushed his glasses up and looked at everyone. "Claire and I decided beforehand that they did not need to be present. She and Ben will meet with them at a time of their choosing."

"Now we come to Claire…" Clarence took a sip of water, gazed around the room before his eyes settled on Claire. His warm eyes reassured her. "Claire, you are the daughter of my heart and Jack, my grandson. I felt that almost from the moment we first met. You were always welcoming, listening to the stories of my past, never irritated or impatient when I dropped by the office. Our Sunday dinners meant the world to me and Jack's antics always made me laugh. Thank you for that. The ranch, the property, and everything on it is yours. In addition, all remaining investments go to you with eighty thousand set aside specifically for Jack's college education. You're the only person I want the ranch to go to. You'll care for it the way it should be cared for, and you won't sell it to those greedy bastard developers. You are a treasure, and I'm forever grateful to you. Don't forget about that other treasure."

Tears rolled down Claire's cheeks at William's first sentence. But when Clarence read that she was getting the ranch and everything, her mouth fell open. She shook her head in disbelief, not noticing that everyone was staring at her.

When Clarence finished, Maggie broke the silence that had fallen on everyone. "That old codger had a soft spot for you, Claire, rightly so. I can't imagine a better person getting this ranch, hon." She cackled and slapped her knee when she observed the dumbfounded look on Claire's face. "Close your mouth before the flies settle inside. They're probably already there considering how long it's been open."

Claire snapped her mouth shut and stood up. "I...I..." Clearing her throat, she tried again. "I'm at a loss." She gave herself a mental shake and mock-scowled at Maggie. "Maggie, you are indeed an old codger as William said." Shaking her head and smiling, she walked over to Maggie who had scooted off the sofa. Claire hugged her. "But a lovable one."

"Oh poo..." She shooed Claire away.

Clarence cleared his throat, putting the papers inside his briefcase then standing up along with Ben and Jackie. "I'll work with Claire to ensure that all paperwork is in order and you get the items as outlined in William's will. Thanks to all of you for being here this afternoon. If there's nothing else, I'll see myself out. Claire, I'll be in touch in a couple of days."

"Thank you Clarence." He nodded at her as he walked to the front door.

Claire said goodbye to Maggie and Jackie who were the next to leave, Maggie chatting nonstop to a brooding Jackie.

Kent spoke up for the first time. "Ben, we're going to stop by your place tomorrow to talk. Since you were the last person to see William alive, we have some questions and need to clarify a few things."

Ben nodded then turned toward Claire. "I've got to talk to Jill and then take care of some work before it gets dark."

"Thanks Ben. I'll walk over to your place in a few minutes to pick up Eddie. It's time I got him home."

Ben's eyebrow shot up. "This is your home."

Claire pulled up short, rubbing her brow. "This is going to take some getting used to."

Chuckling, Ben told her they'd talk about the ranch operations in the coming days, before excusing himself and walking out the back door.

Taking a deep breath, Claire turned and faced Kent and Deputy Hanson.

"Well, well, well." Hanson rocked back on his heels. "This is an interesting turn of events."

Chapter 12

KENT SAID THEY NEEDED TO TALK, so Claire offered them a seat in William's dining room then sat down. "I need to pick up Eddie in about five minutes."

Deputy Hanson leaned forward and pointed his finger at Claire. "You'll leave when we say you can leave…"

"Claire,…" Kent interrupted Deputy Hanson. "Can you tell us again about the night of the thirtieth? You came to William's for dinner."

Ignoring Deputy Hanson, Claire focused solely on Kent. "Yes, Eddie and I arrived at about five in the afternoon. William wanted to see Eddie in his bumblebee costume." She smiled at the memory. "I was there for about ten minutes when Jackie arrived."

Kent's eyebrows rose. "Ben told us she was there. Did she stay with you and William?"

Claire shook her head. "William told me he'd take care of dinner. I didn't realize that meant he'd have Jackie bring it over. I told him I could have brought dinner but he said Jackie liked to help." She paused and frowned. "I offered for Jackie to stay but William said she was always busy. Jackie agreed but now that I think about it, she looked peeved."

"What makes you say that?"

"I'm not sure. William talked about how helpful Jackie was, running errands and driving him to and fro. She said the only place he drove himself was to my office. I'm sure that was an exaggeration, but her tone was… envious, maybe?"

"Well, that's certainly convenient."

Claire stiffened. "Excuse me, Deputy Hanson?"

He smirked. "As we learned today, you had the most to gain by William's death and you conveniently find someone else to blame?"

"I was simply explaining what happened when I went to William's for dinner. I wasn't blaming anyone for anything."

Kent gave a warning look to Deputy Hanson. "Deputy Hanson wasn't accusing you of anything, Claire. We're just trying to understand everything that occurred leading up to William's murder. Please continue."

Claire put her hands in her lap. They were shaking and she didn't want Deputy Hanson to realize that he'd upset her. "We ate dinner and talked about everything and nothing, usual chit chat. After dinner, I put Eddie in his playpen and we went into the living where William showed me his trunk." Claire looked toward the hearth, for the first time noticing that the trunk wasn't there. "I guess he had Ben put it back into the attic."

"What trunk?"

"It's a beautiful old trunk that he said belonged to his great-grandfather, Billy Miner."

Deputy Hanson scoffed. "Billy Miner? Really? That outlaw died in the eighteen hundreds. Everyone knows that."

Claire was shaking her head. "William said he survived and lived another three years. He showed me an old gun that he said was Billy's as well as a cowboy hat." Claire didn't mention the map.

"What happened after that?" Kent asked.

"It was getting late and we went home, probably close to eight."

Deputy Hanson sneered. "You expect us to believe that you didn't know what was in that will and that you were basically getting everything? You are the only one with a clear motive."

Claire shot out of the chair, shaking with anger. "Oh yeah, you got me. I came back here a couple of hours later with my two-year-old son strapped to my back. I had Eddie hold the knife for me and then as soon as William opened the door, I grabbed it from my son and stabbed him in the chest." She held out her hands, wrists together. "Arrest me. But you'd better arrest my son as well, since he was an accomplice." She was breathing hard, near tears.

Now standing as well, Kent placed his hand on her wrists and gently pushed her arms down.

She turned tortured eyes and stared at him but he was staring at the deputy.

"Deputy Hanson owes you an apology," he growled, his icy glare never leaving the Deputy's face.

Hanson's eyes narrowed.

The only sound that registered was her own breathing as the two men faced off.

Taking a deep breath and breaking eye contact with Kent, Deputy Hanson apologized to Claire. "I apologize, ma'am. I shouldn't have accused you in such a manner when you're clearly upset after losing such a close friend."

His emphasis of 'a close friend' grated on Claire's nerves. "Chalk it up to being eager to find Miner's killer."

Claire lowered her eyes, frowning. *Was that an apology or a barely veiled accusation?* Claire pinched the bridge of her nose. A headache was developing. She looked up at the deputy and inclined her head. Stepping around the deputy, she walked to the front door and opened it signaling the end of the conversation. "I need to pick up my son."

Slipping on his sunglasses, Deputy Hanson left.

Kent stopped and looked down at her. "I'm sorry about William, Claire." Without another word, he followed the deputy out the door.

***

"A complaint has been filed against you." Chief Deputy Banner said as soon as Kent sat down in his office. Banner's wiry thin frame and pasty white skin gave some the impression that the Chief Deputy was a pushover or at best, weak. Kent found the opposite to be true. Banner knew the job and performed with equal parts fairness and toughness.

"Don't tell me, Hanson is whining."

Banner spit a stream of tobacco juice into a spittoon on the floor next to his chair and wiped his lip. "Says you're biased where St. John is concerned."

"That's bullshit. He has accused her on more than one occasion with no provocation, no cause, no proof, and he's unwilling to consider anyone else as a suspect."

"From what I understand, she inherited most of William's wealth. She has motive."

Kent nodded. "That's true. So do others. Three people were with William that evening, Claire, Ben Capshaw the foreman, and Jackie Baker, a helper of William's."

"You suppose one of them killed him?"

Kent shrugged. "What I do know is that I need to work with someone who is willing to consider all possibilities, look outside the box, and work as hard and as long as necessary to find William's killer. Hanson didn't even want to observe the autopsy. He wanted to wait for the report. Seriously?"

"Sounds like you want to take him off the case." Elbows on the desk and hands steepled under his chin, he studied Kent.

Kent blew out a breath. "I'm leaning in that direction. Look, he's been in my department for three months, handled that burglary case well enough for his first case, according to Deputy Smith who worked alongside him." He shook his head. "I'm not sure I should have brought him into this murder case. His inexperience is showing. That aggressive attitude and behavior might be needed or expected when out on patrol where he was transferred from but…"

He rubbed his chin then looked at his boss. "This might be too much for him too soon."

Banner leaned back in his seat and stared out the window. He absently scratched his belly before sitting up and spitting into the spittoon once more. He turned his head and pursed his lips as he considered Kent. "You recognize how this will look, especially given the complaint."

Kent nodded.

"I trust your instincts, Kent, that's why you're where you are." He paused and picked up his readers, placed them on his nose and opened a blue folder. After perusing it, he looked up at Kent, his mirth barely contained. "You're getting a short reprieve."

Kent's brows shot up.

"A request came in yesterday. Pablo Gonzalez of the Spurs is evidently getting married and has ten days of activities planned in the hill country and San Antonio leading up to the nuptials at his home in the Dominion on the twenty-third. He has requested increased security during this time. I'm looking for two deputies within the sheriff's office to work with others in Bexar, Gillespie, and Blanco counties to provide said security."

He closed the folder and continued. "Although it's a request, it comes with a very generous donation to the Kendall County Sheriff's Office as well as to the other offices that will be participating. With the positive exposure we'll receive, Sheriff Dean is eager to accept."

"A feather in his cap for sure." Kent grinned. "You could have led with that." He shook his head.

Banner laughed. "I like to watch you squirm."

Kent stood. "I don't squirm." He turned to leave.

"Don't worry about Hanson. He's such a fan of the Spurs, he'll be eager for this temporary assignment. It begins tomorrow."

Kent raised his hand in acknowledgement, whistling under his breath as he opened the door and left.

Already the perfect Tuesday.

Chapter 13

CLAIRE WAS INTERRUPTED FROM PACKING AFTER lunch on Thursday when there was a knock on her door. Rubbing her lower back, she walked to the front door and opened it. "Grace, I'm so glad you're here. Come on in."

"Wow! You've done a lot in just a few days." Grace observed the boxes stacked in one corner of the living room.

Claire scanned her apartment. "There wasn't that much to do actually. The landlord agreed to let me out of my lease when I told him I'd leave the furnishings, including dishes and all. I just had to pack personal things and I'm taking my small appliances." She handed Grace a glass of lemonade.

"Nice. What about the office?"

Claire sighed. "He agreed to give me forty-five days to pack up and move." She scrunched her nose. "I'm still trying to figure out where I'm going to set up. This office was the perfect location." She sighed before sipping her lemonade. "And I'm sorry for putting the website on the back burner for now."

Grace waved it off. "No need to apologize. Things have been crazy."

"That's a good word for it. It's been non-stop. I worked with Clarence to get the beneficiaries the things that William left them. That wasn't too difficult, actually. Paperwork mostly for the transfers. But there is so much legal crap to get through related to the property and all, not to mention a tour of the property from Ben and learning the ins and outs of running a ranch, contacting my clients, the list goes on." Claire brushed the bangs off her forehead. "It's exhausting."

"You do look tired."

Claire stuck her tongue out.

Grace laughed. "Eddie's at day care?"

Claire nodded. "I need to pick him up in…" She checked her watch. "…thirty minutes."

"That's one of the reasons why I'm here. Since you're moving to the ranch tomorrow, why don't I take Eddie for the weekend? You can settle in and we can bring him over on Sunday afternoon."

"Grace, that would be a tremendous help. I was going to ask Jackie to babysit him on Saturday…"

"Jo has already said she'd love to spend time with him, we all would." Grace took one last sip of lemonade. "Why don't you get some things together for him and I'll pick him up."

"Awesome! You said that was one of the reasons you stopped by." Claire led Grace into the bedroom then pulled out Eddie's bag and began packing clothes and diapers while Grace plopped onto the bed.

"Has Kent contacted you at all or revealed anything more about the investigation?"

Claire paused and glanced at Grace before placing Eddie's pajamas in the bag. "Not a word. No news is good news, right?"

"Absolutely. And, by the way, I'm so sorry for blabbing all your business at dinner the other night."

"Don't worry about it, Grace. Kent would have found all that out soon enough. I just never figured that he would consider me a suspect, that I could hurt William." She shook her head. "Deputy Hanson, on the other hand, seems hell-bent on blaming me."

"I don't believe that Kent suspects you. If he's anything like Ethan, and they're exactly alike by the way, he'll figure out what's going on."

"Well, I'm not going to sit here and wait for them to blame me." She zipped Eddie's bag and straightened.

"Claire, you need to leave this to Kent." She took the bag from Claire and they both walked to the front door.

"Why kill William? Why kill him now? Nothing appears to have been stolen, but Ben isn't aware of everything William had. It doesn't make sense to me. I have to go through everything in the house anyway. I'm simply going to be thorough as I do that. Maybe something will jump out at me, look odd or something." She opened the door.

"That doesn't sound bad. Promise me that if you find anything that doesn't make sense, you'll call Kent."

The two women stared at each other, both with determined looks on their faces but for different reasons.

"Oh all right." Claire relented. "I doubt I'll even find anything but I have to try."

Grace laughed. "I never realized how stubborn you are." She gave Claire a quick hug and walked out the door.

Claire took everything to the ranch shortly after Grace left, vowing to come back to clean the apartment on Monday.

She stopped at HEB to stock up on groceries then arrived at the ranch just after four p.m. She'd paid Jill to clean the house and was grateful when she opened the refrigerator and realized that she'd also emptied it and cleaned the shelves. After unloading the groceries and putting them away, she brought the boxes and suitcases inside and put them in the living room.

She had not yet fully explored the house and wanted to become more familiar with it. Walking down a short hallway, she found two bedrooms and a full bathroom. She flipped on the light switch of the first bedroom. Nothing happened. Making a mental note to go through the entire house and draft a list of needed repairs, she walked to the window on the far wall and opened the blinds to let some light in.

She smiled as she watched the chickens run out of the barn. This would be perfect for Eddie. The room had a double bed and a small dresser. The walls were painted a hideous brown and there was nothing hanging on the walls. She would definitely have to paint the room.

Claire groaned when she walked into the second bedroom and turned on the light. It was about the same size as the first bedroom but there was no furniture. Instead, there were file-sized boxes stacked one on top of the other in the middle. Walking to the nearest box, she blew dust off the lid then pulled it off. Inside were stacks of papers. Her shoulders drooped. Going through all the boxes was going to be a chore. Not today. She dropped the lid back on top of the box then turned and walked out. At least the light worked.

She glanced in the bathroom, then walked through the living room to the office on the other side of the front door.

She couldn't even claim organized chaos when she scanned the room. The desk, an old wooden table, was positioned on the left side of the room, covered in papers. An office chair was right behind it. There were three open boxes with papers stuffed inside sitting next to the desk and more boxes stacked on top of each other in the center.

Surely, these boxes and the ones in that bedroom aren't his filing system.

But as her eyes moved from one side of the room to the other, she realized that there were no filing cabinets. In fact, the only other furniture in the office was on the far side of the room. An oversized brown leather chair with multiple coats thrown over it was pushed up against what looked like an antique cabinet of some sort.

Ignoring the desk, she sidestepped the boxes in the center and walked over to the chair, shoving it to the side. The cabinet was a buffet. She gasped when she laid eyes on it. Made of oak, the sideboard buffet was about four feet long and three feet high. There were three up-per dovetailed drawers and a large cabinet below them with two doors for access. The hand-carved details were exquisite and when she looked inside the drawers and cabinet, faded paper of some sort covered the sides. The bottoms were bare wood. It was in excellent condition and reminded Claire of William's trunk. *I'll bet Elizabeth brought this with her along with the trunk.*

Claire paused, frowning. William's trunk. Pulling her cell phone out of her back pocket, she texted Ben asking him if he knew where the trunk was. Twenty seconds later he responded, *headed over there now.*

Claire walked to the kitchen when there was a knock on the back door.

"Come on in, Ben."

The door opened and Ben and Jill stepped inside with Bear.

"Hi Claire. Couldn't wait until tomorrow, huh?" He was smiling as he pulled off his cowboy hat and held it in his hand.

Claire laughed. "I could only come today because Grace took Eddie for the weekend."

"I was planning to bring this to you tomorrow to welcome you, but when we saw your car…"

"Jill, thank you so much. Wow!" She accepted the casserole and set it on the stove. "I'll enjoy it for dinner tonight. And thanks as well for cleaning the place. This is all so overwhelming…"

"My pleasure. Some rooms were a little too…" She gestured with her hands. "…full?"

Claire laughed. "That's a nice way of putting it."

Ben cleared his throat. "I hope this is a good time to bring Bear over. I figure he'd be more comfortable near William's things."

"Of course. This is his home." She knelt down and scratched behind his ears. "Hey Bear, how are you doing, buddy? I'm sure you're missing William, but we hope you'll come to love us as much as you loved him." She kissed his head.

Standing back up, she looked at Ben. "When Eddie and I had dinner with William the night he was killed, he showed me a trunk that he said belonged to his great-grandfather. It was sitting by the fireplace, but it's not there anymore."

Ben was nodding as she spoke. "William had me bring it down from the attic that afternoon. After you

left, I asked him if he wanted me to return it to the attic."
He looked a little sheepish, playing with his cowboy hat.
"I was late getting home and he said it could wait a day
or two." He frowned. "I don't know where it is, come to
think of it."

"Could he have taken it to the attic himself?"

"No, it was pretty heavy, but let me take a look."

As he disappeared through a door by the office,
Claire turned toward Jill. "We haven't really had time to
get to know each other yet. Have you lived in Boerne all
your life?"

Jill shook her head. "I grew up in Dallas, moved
here a few months before I married Ben."

"Really? I was born and raised in California but
lived with my husband in Dallas for a few years. It's too
crowded for me." Claire sighed.

"I was supposed to be here on a job for a year or
so. But when I met Ben at the post office, I knew he was
the man for me so I introduced myself. We married three
months to the day after that."

"That's so romantic."

Jill shrugged, her expression unreadable. "I still miss
the fast pace of Dallas."

Ben returned from the attic.

"I'm sorry Claire but it's not there."

Chapter 14

"THANK YOU FOR COMING OVER THIS late, Kent." Claire had called Kent as soon as Ben and Jill left. While waiting for him to arrive, she went through each room again, looking much more closely for the trunk in case she'd missed it. It was nowhere to be found.

"You were pretty vague on the phone, just saying it had something to do with William's murder." He stepped inside and Claire closed the door behind him.

"Can I get you something to drink? A beer?"

Kent shook his head. He was still in uniform. "Soda?"

"Coming right up. Have a seat in the living room." She walked into the kitchen and grabbed the soda from the fridge and a bottle of water for herself. "Where's your sidekick?" She handed him the can and sat down opposite him on the sofa.

"Special assignment for two weeks."

A flicker of surprise crossed her face as she sipped her water.

"What's going on, Claire?" He looked around. "And where's Eddie?"

"He's spending a long weekend at Ethan and Grace's. They're bringing him home on Sunday." She swallowed more water before placing the bottle on the coffee table. "The trunk I told you about is missing. It was stolen."

He leaned forward and rested his elbows on his knees, the soda held loosely in his hand. His eyes narrowed. "The trunk William said was his great-grandfather's?" Grace nodded. "Are you sure?"

"Yes. When I left that night, it was sitting right next to the fireplace. I spoke with Ben and he said that he brought it down from the attic that afternoon, but William told him he could return it to the attic in the next couple of days."

"And William couldn't have moved it someplace else?"

Claire shook her head. "That trunk is heavy. When he showed it to me, he struggled to pull it from the hearth to the edge of the sofa where he was sitting. But I looked through the entire house just to make sure. It's nowhere to be found."

"Tell me again what was in the trunk."

"He showed me a cowboy hat that supposedly belonged to another gang member. Evidently, the gang wore the same outfit of jeans, black shirt, long black overcoat, and a black mask when they robbed a bank or whatever but they each wore their own cowboy hat. The hat had to be black as well. William said Billy's hat was very distinctive, which is why he switched hats with his buddy...to fool the Rangers into thinking they'd caught Billy. He also showed me an old Colt revolver that he said was Billy's."

"Anything else?"

Claire hesitated. She had not mentioned the map when she initially spoke with Kent and Deputy Hanson.

"Claire?"

Claire sighed. "There were other things in the trunk but he didn't show them to me. I got a quick look when he shoved them aside but I couldn't say what they were. He wanted to show me the hidden compartment at the bottom that he said had the map."

"So a map exists?"

Claire nodded. "He said it's pretty basic and tried to find the treasure ever since he moved here. He even bought this ranch originally because he thought the treasure was somewhere on the property."

"So you've seen the map?"

"Nope, he showed me the compartment, but it was empty. He said the map was someplace safe."

"Here in the house?"

Grace snorted. "If it is, I doubt I'll ever find it." She shook her head. "He has boxes and boxes of papers and everything is so disorganized. I'll start going through things this weekend, but it's going to take time."

Kent stared at Claire.

She frowned as the silence continued. "Do I have a wart on my nose or something?" She swiped her nose.

Kent grinned. "You really believe he's Billy Miner's great-grandson, don't you?"

"Yes I do."

His tone became serious. "If that's the case and there truly is a map to Miner's treasure, then we've just found a motive for William's murder. And if someone stole that trunk because they believe that as well, you could be in danger."

Claire paled and her hand came up to her chest. "I...I..." She shook her head. "That's an assumption. People have been looking for that treasure for decades."

"True. But someone else believes it can be found and took the trunk in the hopes of finding clues. Who else knows about the map?" His stomach growled loud enough for Claire to hear. He smiled at the expression on her face and looked at his watch. "Listen, I haven't eaten since breakfast and I'm starving. Have you eaten?" Claire shook her head. "Why don't we grab a bite at the Hungry Horse and talk about this some more. The girls are having a sleepover with friends so I don't have to get home for them."

"Kent..."

"Just dinner Claire. I need more info about all of this for my investigation and we have to eat, right?"

Claire's shoulders relaxed. "All right. Let me grab my purse. I'll follow you."

Twenty minutes later, they walked into the Hungry Horse and got in line to order. The Hungry Horse was a comfort-food dining joint where you ordered your meal at the front counter from a massive menu on the back wall before finding a table and waiting for your order to be called. Many people sitting at the tables called a greeting out to Kent who responded with a wave, and the couple in line in front of them pulled him into a conversation about the state of the economy.

Claire's stomach growled as scents of turkey and mashed potatoes with gravy greeted her. Well, she couldn't actually smell the mashed potatoes, but she'd enjoyed their turkey dinner before and was imagining it. She licked her lips as she studied the menu. The conversation Kent was having flowed over her without distinction as did the various conversations in the room. She smiled when a little girl giggled, then jumped when someone put a hand on her shoulder.

Catching a whiff of the stench of cigarettes, she spun around. "Lenny, hi. Oh my gosh you startled me."

"Sorry Ms. St. John. I followed you in here, had to talk to you. After my wife...you're a single mom..." He paused, shaking his head. "Tried to find you a couple of days ago, but your office and apartment have been dark."

"I'm sorry, Lenny, it's been a chaotic week. You mentioned your wife?" He was shaking his head rapidly from side to side, eyes darting everywhere. Claire frowned. He looked more bedraggled than usual and he was wringing his hands, clearly distraught. She placed her hand on his arm. "Are you all right?"

Lenny lowered his voice to a whisper. Claire leaned in, trying not to grimace as his breath overwhelmed her senses. "I can't talk here, too many people. But I was there, I saw."

"Saw what? What are you talking about?" Brow furrowed, Claire was whispering now as well. She tilted her head as she tried to understand Lenny.

"Can't talk."

"Listen, I'll be in my office Monday morning. Stop by first thing and we'll talk."

Lenny chewed on his lip before nodding. "Monday morning." Without another word, he turned and shuffled out the door.

Claire was still trying to process what had just happened when Kent called her over to place their order. There were only a couple of tables available so by mutual consent they wove a path past the tables and made their way to the corner booth.

"I just had the strangest conversation with one of my clients."

Kent looked around. "Anyone I know?"

"I doubt it, and he left anyway. Weird." She shrugged. "I'm meeting with him on Monday." She leaned in toward Kent, forcing him to do the same because she spoke in a soft voice. "He's the reason why I quit smoking."

"Really?"

"I was down to one or two cigarettes a day, but he smells like a cigarette factory, reeks of it actually. I don't want to end up like that with Eddie imagining that his mom is rich because she smells like smoke and thus must own the tobacco companies." She shook her head and grinned when Kent laughed.

They chit-chatted about his girls and school while they waited for their dinner. Claire remembered how easy it was to talk to Kent.

"How is your mom?" After Kent's wife walked away from their marriage and their kids, Kent had moved back into the family ranch with his mom who had helped with the girls. Diagnosed with dementia, her condition had been worsening when Claire first met her a few months ago.

"I moved her to the Angel Assisted Living facility outside of Boerne six weeks ago."

"Oh, Kent." She placed her hand on his forearm.

He looked down at her hand and sighed. "It was the right thing to do. She was wandering outside the house and it was getting too hard to care for her. I'm grateful for the seclusion of the ranch and all my workers there…

her wandering could have been much worse." He shook himself and raised his eyes to Claire's. "But she's thriving there with all the activities. I visit her a couple times a week and take the girls with me frequently."

"Thank you for telling me." She removed her hand from his arm. "So are you seeing anyone?"

Kent's blinked, startled.

Claire blushed. "I said that out loud? I'm sorry, none of my business." She fiddled with the fork and knife on the table.

"I'm not seeing anyone. How can I when someone else is still on my mind?"

Claire's eyes shot to Kent's and time seemed to stop.

"Order for Kent."

Claire swallowed and leaned back in her seat. Kent continued to stare at her in that intense way that could always make her melt inside.

"Order for Kent."

Kent slid out of the booth and went to the front while Claire fanned herself. He returned a couple of minutes later, setting both trays down.

Claire made a big show of exclaiming over the food and picked up her fork, digging into the meal.

Kent tucked into his meal as well. About half way through, he set his fork down. "Who else has knowledge of the trunk or the map?"

Claire shrugged. "I don't know. Ben obviously, since he brought it down from the attic. I had lunch with Grace at Barkley's a while ago. We spoke about the trunk and William's relationship to Billy Miner. Maggie and Jackie were there as well. Maggie said he'd been telling that tale for years to anyone who would listen and no one believed him. But Gail was serving us and there were people at tables nearby. Anyone could have overheard the conversation, I suppose."

"Did you mention the map to anyone?"

Claire shook her head. "Jackie talked about the treasure being spread throughout the hill country. I told her that William said Billy Miner moved it to one location but I didn't mention the map at all. And quite honestly, I'm not sure the map would even do us any good. William knew his family's story better than anyone and had the map yet he couldn't find the treasure."

"Good point." He finished his meal and moved the tray to the side. "But the fact remains that someone wants to find the treasure and they assume that something inside the trunk will help them or they wouldn't have taken it. Nor would they have killed William."

Claire chewed her lip again. "I still don't understand why William was killed now. Why not a year ago? Two years ago?"

Kent shook his head as he stood and assisted Claire out of the booth. "I intend to find out."

They walked out of the Hungry Horse and to their vehicles which were parked next to each other.

Kent stopped at Claire's car and turned her to face him. "If it's all right with you, I'd like to help you go through those boxes."

"Surely you have better things to do than help me go through old boxes? And what about the case? Isn't there stuff you should be doing for that?"

"The investigation is on-going but this is part of it now as well. Look, I'm not picking up the girls until two tomorrow afternoon. I can spend the morning helping you. I'll work on other aspects of the case tonight and in between the girl's schedule this weekend."

Claire pursed her lips, considering. "Is eight o'clock too early?"

"I'll bring the breakfast tacos." He reached over to her car door and opened it. "Keep your doors locked at the ranch and be careful, Claire."

Chapter 15

UNABLE TO SLEEP, CLAIRE WAS UP at five thirty. She had not considered how she would feel sleeping in William's house, where he lived and where he died. She didn't know where in the house the murder took place, and the house had been cleaned of any evidence of his death prior to his celebration of life, for which she was grateful…but still.

Dressed in an old sweatshirt and sweatpants with her hair braided and hanging down her back, she made a pot of coffee then filled a cup. After picking up the cup and her bag containing her laptop along with various documents Clarence had given her including the title to the property that was now in her name, bank accounts, and a checkbook, she walked to the office.

Halting at the door, she took a deep breath then marched inside. Organization was her middle name. She would tackle the paperwork on the desk first. Placing her bag on the desk chair, she pushed some papers to the side and set her coffee down.

She dove into the papers, sorting and stacking them, including a pile for miscellaneous items that needed further review. Paying the current bills was a priority though, so after moving her bag to the floor, she sat down in the chair and pulled out her laptop. William wasn't technologically savvy, so the first thing she did was register for online banking. She set up the online accounts for all bills, carefully reviewing previous payments and amounts due.

For local bills, she planned to take the payments to the local offices so she could introduce herself. Pulling the checkbook from her bag, she wrote the checks and set them aside. For the non-local bills like the three credit cards he had, she scheduled online payments.

Straightening, she rolled her head before glancing at her watch. Seven-forty-five. She didn't realize how much time had passed. Picking up her empty coffee cup, she returned to the kitchen. She'd just poured another cup when the front doorbell rang. Eight o'clock on the nose. Kent was always punctual.

She unlocked and opened the door. "Good morning."

"I'm glad you locked your front door." Claire rolled her eyes. With a mischievous look, he stepped inside and handed her a paper bag. "Breakfast is served."

Claire put her nose in the bag and inhaled. "Mmmmmm, bacon. I'm starving." She led the way to the kitchen and set the bag down. "Help yourself to coffee." Grabbing two paper plates and napkins, she gestured to the stools at the island. She ripped open the bag and set it between the plates, six tacos spread between them.

Kent sat down next to her. "Two bacon and egg, two chorizo and egg, two potato, cheese and egg." Picking up a chorizo and egg taco, he unwrapped the foil and took a big bite.

Grabbing a bacon and egg taco, she wasted no time devouring it.

As soon as they finished, they made their way to the office. Kent stopped at the entrance. "There's a table in the center of the room?" He turned to Claire, grinning. "What time did you get up?"

"Five-thirty. Couldn't sleep." They walked to the table and she showed him what she'd done. "Just basic organization of the paperwork before I tackled the bills, put everything online. They're all his personal bills. I asked Ben for the ranch financials and we're meeting in his office in the barn tomorrow morning to go over that stuff. He's showing me the property first."

"I'm impressed." Kent looked around. "This actually doesn't look too bad. What would you like me to do first?"

Claire laughed. "You haven't seen the guest bedroom yet." Pointing to the boxes on the far side of the buffet, she added, "If you'll work on those boxes, I'll finish organizing the table then I'll tackle the boxes that are right here. I assume the boxes here in the office are the more current stuff. At least I'm hoping that's the case."

She chuckled. "I've ordered two filing cabinets and a shredder. They should arrive on Monday. Oh, if anything looks like it doesn't fit, add it to the miscellaneous pile on top of the buffet and we'll go through it last."

Kent nodded and walked over to the four boxes stacked on top of each other and opened the first one.

A companionable silence fell as they got to work.

Opening the third box in his stack, Kent looked at the first document and frowned. "Claire, didn't you say that a developer had been trying to buy the ranch?"

Claire looked up from the paper in her hand and nodded.

He shuffled through the box. "Looks like this entire box is about their efforts."

"William never gave me details although I'm not surprised he kept the information." Distracted, she looked back down at the paper in her hand.

"Some firm in Dallas, called…" he paused as he pulled the first document out. "…Judson Development."

The paper in Claire's hand fluttered to the floor as she stood.

Flipping to the next page, he cleared his throat. "Holy Cow! They offered him a ridiculous amount of money. I mean, this ranch is worth a lot but…" he paused again when he glanced up, her pale face catching his eye. With the document still in his hand, he walked over to her. "You look like you're about to pass out." Pushing her down on to the chair, he crouched in front of her. "What is it? You look like you've seen a ghost."

She was shaking her head. "It can't be." Her eyes were filled with pain. "Who from the company made the offer?"

Looking down at the document, he flipped through the pages until he got to the last page. "The representative was Michael St. John."

Through dry lips, Claire mumbled, "My husband."

Chapter 16

KENT HELPED CLAIRE INTO THE LIVING room where she sank onto the sofa. Stepping away from her, he returned a moment later with a glass that contained amber liquid.

"Drink this."

She took the glass then mechanically brought it to her lips and took a sip, promptly coughing and gasping. "It's not even ten o'clock and you gave me whiskey?" She set the glass on the coffee table and glared at him.

"You were in shock." Pulling his other arm from behind him, he handed her a bottle of water then sat down beside her. "You never told me much about your marriage."

Claire swallowed some water then sighed. "You know that we met and dated when I was attending Cal Poly in San Luis Obispo. He was a guest speaker in a real estate finance class I took." Kent nodded. "Michael was twelve years older than I and was a rising star in his real estate development firm. We married as soon as I graduated and I moved to Dallas, worked for a financial firm there. Over the course of a few years, we tried to have a child but I had three miscarriages in five years."

Kent covered her hand with his. She looked down at their hands and a ghost of a smile crossed her face. "We kind of gave up after that. Michael got busier with work and spent less and less time with me. We grew apart." She rubbed her face. "I don't mean to sound like I'm blaming him. It takes two and I was busy with my work as well. The difference, I guess, is that I followed through with things."

Claire glanced around the living room before dropping her gaze. "If I said I'd meet him somewhere, I did. If I said dinner was going to be ready at a certain time, it was. But those last, I don't know, six or seven months he stopped trying. I'd have dinner ready and he wouldn't show, wouldn't even call to say he had to work late. If we were going to meet for a drink or dinner after work, I'd show up and he wouldn't. I thought he was having an affair." She shrugged.

"What did Michael do for Judson?"

"He spearheaded multi-state real estate projects in large cities so he traveled a lot. And he'd be gone for long periods at a time, coming home once a month or so for a long weekend. Sometimes I'd travel to him. He was in Boerne when I found out I was pregnant with Eddie."

"Why was Michael in Boerne?"

"What do you mean? He was working on a project that evidently involved trying to buy William's property."

"You said his projects were in large cities. So why small-town Boerne? Why this project?"

Claire frowned. "Michael was good at his job. Maybe they were having problems and he was the best person to seal the deal."

"Did he ever talk to you about that project?"

"He never talked to me about any of his projects." Her eyes narrowed as memories flooded in. "As I recall, I never visited him while he was working here in Boerne. He'd come home to Dallas for a long weekend and that was only early in the project. He didn't come home at all the last couple of months, said he was too busy trying to finish the job. I told him about the pregnancy via FaceTime."

Kent paused and looked toward the kitchen. Seconds turned into minutes.

"What are you thinking?"

He returned his focus to her. "Multiple months is a long time to be here trying to buy William's property."

"He might have been working on other stuff at the same time?" She shrugged. "William told me that the ranchers on either side of him sold their properties and that the developers were planning to build a community of homes with stores and restaurants. He said it was ridiculous to believe anyone would buy this far out or come here to go to a restaurant. He thought his neighbors were greedy fools. William was the last holdout."

Kent stood up and began pacing. He stopped in front of the fireplace and stared at the portrait of Billy Miner that was sitting on the mantle. "So it's possible Michael handled those other sales."

Claire watched him as he paced, not bothering to respond.

"Often times when a developer buys multiple properties and there's a holdout, the developer will begin construction around the holdout property. They use that as a means to pressure the property owner to sell. But there's been no development on the other two properties. Why?"

He turned to look at her. "Did he still have a job when he returned to Dallas?"

"He appeared nervous when he got home, jittery. At the time, I didn't attribute it to fear of being fired. It didn't cross my mind at all, actually." She scowled. "That doesn't sound very good, does it?" She shook her head. "He never said he was fired."

"Was he assigned to a new project?"

"No clue. He went into work as usual."

"At least he had something to look forward to." At Claire's questioning glance, he added, "Eddie."

"I was seven months pregnant when Michael died."

"He never met his son? I'm sorry, Claire."

"Don't be. He wasn't thrilled when I told him I was pregnant and he wasn't home for most of the pregnancy. I'm pretty sure that he didn't want a child anymore. And the auto accident occurred just a month after he returned home."

Reaching for her bottle of water, she didn't notice Kent's look of alarm.

Chapter 17

It was a cool Sunday morning for November when Claire toured the property with Ben on horseback. Her mount, Pocahontas, was a three-year-old pinto with a calm disposition. Having grown up with horses in California, she relished the opportunity to ride again.

"William had the entire property fenced in when he moved here." At Claire's look of surprise, he smiled. "It was a daunting task, but it was worth it. Barbed wire fencing used to be in the front, but William wanted the entry to be a little more grand and secure. As you've seen, it's eight feet tall and made of concrete blocks covered with stucco. The sides and back fencing are barbed wire, six feet high."

"Have you had any problems with break-ins or anything like that?"

Ben shook his head. "None. The two houses, barn, bunkhouse and corrals are about a quarter mile from the road and are situated in the middle of the property." His tone was that of a teacher and Claire appreciated the details he offered without having to be asked. She learned about the irrigated pasture land, stock ponds, septic tanks, hay, and cattle as they rode.

She marveled at the terrain they passed—from the wheat-colored grasses and various bushes to the occasional stately oak trees that currently offered shade to many cows. She stopped periodically to take it all in.

They had traveled about two-thirds along the perimeter when Claire observed the change in terrain. They were climbing a hill and the oak trees and some cedar trees were becoming much more prevalent. She had to duck in a few places to avoid hitting low-hanging branches.

Claire stopped to look across the barbed-wire fence to the property on the other side. "Ben, I know that property was sold a couple years back. Do you know what's going on there?"

Ben glanced to his left. "I'm not sure. A buddy of mine was a ranch hand there. He said all the livestock was sold and he, along with the other ranch hands, were let go." He nudged his bay forward. "When we reach the bottom of the hill, we'll be at the back of the property."

Claire nodded, still looking beyond the fence. *Did Michael's company really buy that property?*

They hadn't traveled more than one hundred yards when Claire spotted a large opening on the right. All trees had been removed, and there appeared to be several large holes with mounds of dirt next to each. The holes were about twenty-five feet apart, each surrounded by a small barricade made of two-by-fours. Sprinkled throughout the area were clumps of weeds and grass.

She stopped again. "Ben wait." She swung her leg off and jumped down. "What are these holes?" She walked toward them to get a look at how far down they went.

"Don't go any closer, Claire. It's not entirely stable."

Claire turned, eyebrows raised. "What is this?"

Ben sighed and dismounted. He led her over to the nearest hole, inching as close to the barricade as he dared. "William got it in his mind that treasure was buried here. We spent weeks clearing this area and digging."

She shook her head in disbelief. "He told me he believed the treasure might be on the property. I didn't realize he'd actually searched for it. How far down does each hole go?"

"They vary in depth. The deepest is about forty feet."

Claire rubbed her face with one hand. "I...I...I don't even know what to say." She peeked over the edge of the hole they were standing next to. "What led him to search for treasure here? And how did he decide how deep to dig each hole?" She straightened and turned toward Ben. "Please tell me there aren't any more areas like this on the property."

Ben shook his head. "After we dug the last hole, the one that's the deepest, he gave up. Never tried again." They returned to the horses.

"When did all of this take place?"

Ben rubbed his chin. "Going on five years, I suppose."

"Why weren't the holes ever filled in?" Claire swung into the saddle.

Ben mounted the bay. "Too many other priorities and we don't get back here too often. We check the fence line using drones and only come here if repairs are needed."

"These holes are a hazard. I want them filled. Hire extra people if you have to so that the regular work can continue. And using drones to inspect a property of this size is smart but I still want a ride-by of the entire perimeter on a horse the first of every month."

When they finished the tour, Claire looked at Ben with fresh eyes. "I never realized how big this operation is. I'm impressed Ben."

Clearing his throat, Ben led her into the office in the barn. "Thanks. It's a real team effort. You said you wanted to look at some financials on your own first." He picked up a ledger and a folder, and handed them to Claire. "This will give you an overview of the operation. I'm more than happy to meet with you whenever you'd like to go over details."

"Thanks for the tour, and for all of this. I had a great time."

Claire spent the next few hours going over the information Ben had provided, satisfied with how he was managing the operation and eager to learn more.

After Ethan and Grace brought Eddie home, she spent the evening showing him his new home including his very own bedroom. Her intent was to settle back into a routine with him. So after a macaroni and cheese dinner, she gave him a bath and put him to bed.

Having toured the property, she felt safer and more comfortable in the house. Nevertheless, Eddie still slept in her bedroom.

Chapter 18

AFTER DROPPING EDDIE OFF AT DAYCARE and cleaning her apartment, Claire was ready to start the new week. She stowed her cleaning supplies in her car and locked it before entering her office from its back door.

Setting her bag next to her desk, Claire unlocked the front door. She'd just opened her computer when the front door crashed against the wall. Claire jumped up, her eyes flying to her office door. She couldn't decide whether to see who was there or flee out the back, Kent's warning flashing in her mind.

Before she could decide, Lenny stumbled in. More disheveled than usual, his jeans were covered in dirt, his tennis shoes were filthy—was that blood?—and he wore a long, black raincoat. She briefly wondered about the raincoat when the sky was clear, but the bloody handprint smeared on her door caught her attention.

Lenny was gasping, his pale face pinched in pain.

"Lenny!"

He took three quick steps toward her then fell, his shoulder catching the corner of her desk causing him to flip onto his back as he landed with a thud. He groaned as he writhed on the floor.

"Lenny!" Claire raced around her desk and knelt down beside him.

She opened his coat, paling at the sight of the blood bubbling up from a wound in his chest. "Oh my God." She pulled off her cardigan, moved his hand out of the way and applied pressure to the wound with both of her hands. Tears were streaming down her face. "Lenny! What happened? Who did this to you?"

His head stopped moving and he looked at Claire who was focused on his wound. When he grabbed her left wrist with his bloody hand, her eyes flew to his.

"I was there."

His whispered words barely registered. "What?" She leaned closer to his face, turning her head to the side slightly so she could hear him better.

He gasped and his breathing became more labored. "The night he was murdered." He coughed as Claire turned to stare at him in shock. "Behind a tree out front." He groaned, a long wheezing sound.

"Stay with me, Lenny. I don't understand what you mean." Claire was breathing hard, trying to control her emotions, trying to understand what he was saying.

He blinked a few times. "Followed you. You left. Fell asleep. Woke…later. Dark out. Saw someone."

"Who? William? Inside his house?"

Lenny's breathing slowed and his words were slurring. "Walked inshide, lightsh went off. Shaw flash. He… She… came outshide with…, thlought heard me…" He gasped for air. "Shorry, Evie, couldn't plotect…"

"Lenny, hang on." She stood and reached across him for her phone that was sitting on the edge of her desk. Her hands were shaking as she dialed nine-one-one.

After providing the address, she set the phone down beside her. She continued applying pressure on the wound. "Help is on the way, Lenny. They'll be here any minute. Hang on." She glanced at him. His eyes were glassy and he wasn't breathing. She placed her finger on the carotid artery at his neck. No pulse.

No!

Beginning CPR, she lost track of time. She didn't hear the sirens, didn't realize anyone had arrived until a first responder tapped her on the shoulder.

"Move away, ma'am."

Startled, Claire scrambled away until her back slammed against the door to her office. She pulled her knees up to her chest and folded her arms on top of them. Her jaw was slack as she stared at his body.

She had no idea how long she'd been sitting there when Ethan squatted down next to her and touched her knee.

"Claire?"

She blinked a few times before focusing on Ethan. Only then did she become aware of her surroundings. Outside, the sirens blared. Her small office was bathed in the flashing orange lights from the ambulance. The scrape of a chair and the snap of latex gloves drew her eyes toward her desk and back to Lenny. One paramedic was kneeling next to him administering CPR, and the other was taking vitals. Two police officers inspected the crowded space.

Ethan searched her face. "Are you hurt?"

"Huh? Um, no." She looked down at her hands noticing the blood for the first time. "It's Lenny's. I couldn't stop the bleeding." Tears pooled in her eyes.

A commotion in her foyer caused both to look up as Kent burst into the room. He took in the scene then his eyes fell on Claire. Ethan stood and the two men spoke in low tones. After a moment, Ethan went to speak with the paramedics and the officers and Kent knelt in front of her.

He tucked a strand of hair behind her ear. "Come on. Let's get you cleaned up."

Kent guided her into the bathroom, where she looked in the mirror. Partially dried blood covered both hands, and her white silk blouse had smears of blood across the front. At some point, she'd wiped her cheek which also sported a streak of blood. Swallowing multiple times, she looked at Kent through the mirror. He reached beyond her and turned on the tap.

Once she was done, Kent lowered the lid of the toilet and had Claire sit down. "Your office is now a crime scene and is being cordoned off. What do you need from it and I'll get it for you?"

"My laptop and notepad that are on my desk, um, the laptop bag sitting next to my chair." Her brows furrowed.

"Your purse?"

"My wallet and stuff are in the laptop bag.... How long before I'll be able to get back into the office?"

"I'm not sure. A day or two, maybe more."

Claire rubbed her temple in an attempt to hold off the headache that was forming. "In that case, I'll need the three files that are in the file drawer on the left side of the desk."

"I'll be right back. Ethan needs to talk to you."

Claire nodded.

A few moments later, Kent and Ethan walked in, Ethan standing in front of Claire and Kent standing at the door.

"Claire, do you know that man?"

Claire looked at Ethan. "Yes. His name is Lenny Crater. He's a new client. I'd only met with him three times."

"Why would he come here in that condition? Did you have a meeting with him today?"

Rubbing her lip with her thumb, she looked at Ethan. "Sort of. I…" She shifted her gaze to Kent. "When we had dinner at the Hungry Horse on Friday, do you remember when I told you that I had a strange conversation with one of my clients? You were talking with a couple of people while we were waiting in line."

Kent nodded.

"Lenny was that client. He said he'd been trying to reach me and needed to talk."

"Did he say what he wanted to talk about?"

Claire returned her gaze to Ethan. "He said he couldn't talk at the restaurant. I assumed it was about his finances. He'd been in the Army, was medically discharged, and was investing most of his pay. He said he didn't need much cash. I told him to come by today first thing. He was nervous though, and said 'I saw' which seemed strange."

"Saw what?"

Her hand flew to her mouth as she met Kent's gaze. "He was there the night William died."

Chapter 19

"TELL US EVERYTHING." ETHAN HAD TAKEN out a notepad and was preparing to jot down whatever Claire said.

A look passed between Kent and Ethan. "With Lenny's murder now tied to William's murder, Ethan and I will be working the case together."

"Okay." She rubbed her hands on her pants. "Lenny said he was at William's the night of the murder, hiding behind a tree out front. At some point, he fell asleep and when he woke up, night had fallen. His speech was a little garbled but I could still understand him. He said he watched someone walk inside and then the lights went out. There was a flash and then whoever it was walked back outside. Lenny believed that person heard him."

"Was it a man? Could Lenny identify him?"

"He wasn't sure. What he told me was between gasps and was much more abbreviated than what I just conveyed. Oh, he also mentioned a woman, Evie. It sounded like he was sorry he couldn't protect her."

Ethan jotted on the notepad before looking at Kent. "What did you discover out at the Miner place?"

"There was no evidence of a break-in. Either the front door was unlocked or the killer had a key."

"He could have entered from the back door by the kitchen," Claire offered.

Kent shook his head. "Unlikely. That door faces the barn and other buildings all of which have external lights, a much higher risk of detection. The gate was in working order and had not been tampered with, so the killer either had access or entered the property on foot."

"The front has an eight foot privacy wall. How would anyone get over it?"

Kent looked at Ethan and shrugged. "We're still trying to figure that out."

"The front and back property lines are only a half mile or so long, and the fences around the rest of the property are barbed wire. Maybe the killer went in through the side." Claire suggested.

"That's possible but difficult to determine. Claire, I'd like to follow you to your place so I can confirm whether or not Lenny was there."

Ethan stayed behind while Kent followed Claire to the property.

As soon as they arrived, Kent began walking around the area near the house while Claire headed to the back door. Opening it, she hesitated. Taking a few deep breaths, she stepped inside, pausing to listen for any sound. Not hearing anything, she peered into the living room then rushed through the kitchen to her bedroom. Locking the bathroom door, she prepared to shower.

After getting cleaned up and changing, Claire found Kent sitting in a rocker on the porch drinking a soda. She sat down in the rocker next to him.

He tipped the drink toward her. "I helped myself." Taking a sip, he set the can on the ground by the rocker. "Ethan called. Lenny was pronounced dead at the hospital."

Claire pressed her lips together and looked up at the sky before dropping her gaze to look across the driveway. "Did you find anything?"

"Do you see the second oak from the left, the one that is directly across from the living room window?"

"That big one?"

Kent nodded. "You said Lenny smoked."

"Yes. I don't know what brand but he crushed a cigarette outside my office one day. It had a brown butt."

Kent reached down to the ground and picked up a baggie. Inside were the remains of five cigarettes, all with brown butts. "The natural grass and brush behind the tree is flattened."

"Lenny said that he fell asleep."

"Could have been him, could have been a deer."

"A deer that smoked?"

Kent shook his head, smiling. "Do any of the ranch hands smoke?"

Claire nodded. "I've only seen one smoke, but he's always in the back. I've never seen him out front."

"I'll request an autopsy and DNA testing on Lenny. We'll pull DNA off the cigarettes to confirm a match." Kent stood. Claire followed suit. "I should have told you this before you moved in, but you need to change the locks on the house and change all existing gate codes. Only give gate access and house keys to essential personnel."

He was standing close to her, close enough that the heat radiating off him warmed her skin more than the shower had. She stared into his eyes. Licking her dry lips, she swayed toward him. Time slowed down.

"I'll make those arrangements for you tomorrow and I'm having a patrol car drive past your property every hour until I can assign someone to stay here with you."

She stepped back from him. "I don't need a babysitter. Nor do I need anyone to arrange…" she held up both hands signaling quotes "…anything for me. And having a patrol drive by every hour? That's ridiculous and a serious waste of resources."

"Claire…"

She held up her hand. "I'm perfectly fine here."

Kent's hands were fisted at his sides. "So Eddie's perfectly fine here as well, because William wasn't."

Claire reeled back, her posture sagging. "If I thought we were in danger, we'd leave."

Kent placed his hands on her shoulders. "Claire, I don't believe you're safe. You need to take precautions." He dropped his hands and walked past her and down the stairs. "I'll be back later."

"What do you mean?" Jogging down the stairs, she caught up to him as he opened the door to his truck.

"I'm staying here for a few nights until other arrangements can be made."

"What? That's ridiculous. You have a ranch to run. You have two daughters."

"Ginger and Louise can stay with Ethan and Grace and my foreman is extremely good at his job."

Claire opened her mouth but Kent put a finger over it before she could say anything.

"You can come stay at my ranch if you'd prefer. Those are your choices."

Claire glared at him, breathing heavily.

He stood there, watching her.

"Fine. But you have no say in what I do during the day or where I go." She crossed her arms.

"As long as you keep me informed of your whereabouts."

"You can be a real ass."

"So that's a yes?" He grinned at her.

Claire huffed.

He climbed into his truck and rolled down the window.

"In keeping with your dictates, I'm picking Eddie up from daycare later."

Kent gave her a little salute then drove away.

While part of her seethed at his overbearing attitude, another part of her was relieved.

Chapter 20

CLAIRE KEPT HERSELF PREOCCUPIED WITH NOTI-FYING clients that she'd need to conduct meetings with them via video conferencing until she could find a new office space. She was getting ready to head over to Ben's office when the phone rang.

"Hi Claire, it's Jackie."

"Hi Jackie. How are you?"

"I'm okay, I guess. Still having a hard time with William…"

"We miss him every day. What can I do for you?"

"Well, work has kept me busy, of course, but not busy enough to keep my mind off everything. I haven't seen Eddie in a while and was hoping I could spend some time with him now and then, pick him up from day care, that sort of thing."

"Jackie, that's a great idea! He enjoys spending time with you."

"Great. Um, I can pick him up today if you'd like and bring him home."

"I'm picking him up today, but I'll swing by the school and drop off my spare car seat and you can pick him up tomorrow."

"His car seat, of course…that sounds great. Anytime you're in a bind, just give me a call. I'm happy to help."

"I really appreciate that. I'll be there in a little while."

Why didn't I think of that?

Claire picked up the ledger Ben had given her and headed over to his office to discuss a few ranch-related matters.

She was about to rap on the partially open door before entering when she heard loud voices.

"We can't afford it, Jill, I already told you that."

"That's what you always say. I haven't had a new dress in weeks and this one is perfect."

Claire peeked inside the room.

Ben half-sat/half-leaned against his desk while Jill stood between his legs, pouting. She reached up and kissed him while her hand, which had been resting on his shoulder, began to slide down. "Just this one perfect dress. I'll make it worth your while."

He stopped her progress and looked at her, one eyebrow raised. Relenting, he shook his head. "You can get me to say yes easier than our daughter, which isn't saying much."

"So I can get it?"

"Just this one dress, nothing more, and I'm taking you dancing this weekend so I can see it on you."

Jill rained kisses over his face. "That sounds wonderful, but don't forget I'm driving to Dallas this weekend to visit friends. I leave on Saturday and I'll be home Sunday or Monday. It's just you and…"

Claire took a step back, intending to leave, when she accidentally stepped near a chicken, causing it to protest loudly. Claire froze, squeezing her eyes shut and cringing. Shaking her head, she rapped on the door.

"Come in," called Ben.

Claire pushed open the door. "Hi Ben, Jill." She paused on the threshold. "I'm sorry to interrupt…"

Ben waved her in. He'd returned to his office chair and Jill was standing next to him, hand on his shoulder. Her body was rigid as she stared at Claire.

"I just wanted to return the ledger. I have a few questions but we can talk about them later."

Ben took the ledger. "We can go over them now if you'd like."

Jill's unblinking stare unnerved her. Claire swallowed, confusion flickering across her face, then shook her head. "I'm headed to town shortly to pick up Eddie. Perhaps tomorrow, I'll text you. Sorry to interrupt."

Later that day, Eddie was over the moon when Kent arrived. The two played together while Claire made dinner, although Kent seemed subdued. The rest of the evening felt too much like a family enjoying time together.

I need to set some boundaries.

After tucking Eddie into bed in her room, she sat down on the sofa in the living room next to Kent.

"Asleep?"

Claire smiled. "Before his head hit the pillow." She paused then pressed her lips together, a slight frown on her face. "Kent…"

He held up his hand to stop her. "Before you go where I know you're headed, I need to talk to you about William, the case…and Michael."

"Michael?"

"After our conversation the other day, I did some research and also made a phone call to a cop friend of mine in Dallas. I asked him for information about the company where Michael worked."

"Why?"

"Call it intuition. I was concerned about the things you told me." He took a deep breath and let it out. "I discovered that Michael did handle the sale of the properties on either side of William. They were bought at prices well above market value."

Claire frowned. "Where are you going with this?" Crossing her arms, her hands cupped her elbows as she absently tapped her foot.

"Did William ever mention Michael to you?"

Claire shook her head. "He just referred to the developers as those 'greedy bastards' or those 'damn developers'. He never mentioned anyone by name."

"Based on the date each contract was drawn up and when it was signed, the other two property owners sold within two weeks of Michael's arrival in town. Now there was work involved until the properties closed but his work efforts were fairly minimal at that point and they closed quickly since they were cash deals. After those sales closed, I believe Michael was trying to befriend William with the goal of getting him to sell. Perhaps he even learned about William's history."

Claire closed her eyes, trying to remember. "I suppose that's possible. Michael would have loved William and his family history." A small smile crossed her lips before she opened her eyes and looked at Kent. "What does this have to do with anything?"

"I don't think Judson had any intention of building on these properties. My friend called me this afternoon.

It isn't common knowledge, but the company is actually listed under the maiden name of the CEO's wife."

She chewed on her lip.

"Claire, the CEO is Robert Smalley, the great-grandson of Ian Smalley. He was the gang member in the Miner gang that ratted out William's great-grandfather."

Chapter 21

Mid-July 1878

"Billy, your wound isn't properly healed yet."

Billy Miner looked at the woman who had saved his life after the ambush. Elizabeth Swanson wasn't what one would describe as beautiful. Sturdy, kind, dependable were the first words that came to mind. Her long brown hair was in its customary bun at the back of her head and her pale blue eyes were the only assets worth noting on her rugged face. She was short and a little plump but she was strong and she could handle a gun. To him, she was an angel.

After leaving Jimmy in the barn, Billy had traveled north and east quite a distance. He'd pushed Rail, his horse, hard wanting to get as far from Boerne as possible, eventually slowing to a walk to allow him some rest. Riding off the main road, he guided Rail past bushes and trees, staying to the shade as much as possible. The sun was baking him and with no wind, there was no respite.

He had no idea how far he'd gone, but he was getting weaker and wasn't sure how much longer he'd remain conscious. The sun was going to set soon. Billy needed to find help quickly. He crested a hill and spotted a dwelling below with smoke curling toward the sky from a chimney. Just beyond, a small barn sat next to a creek. There were no other dwellings within sight. As he scanned the distance, he figured the next town, Kendalia, was still a good day's ride.

He was interrupted from his musings by the scrape of the barn door opening. A woman walked out carrying something. She closed the door and walked to the house before disappearing inside.

Gritting his teeth to will the dizziness away, he slowly made his way down the hill. His right arm hanging at his side was nearly useless at this point so he steered Rail with his knees and pulled his gun from its holster, holding it with his left hand and resting it on his leg. He wasn't sure he'd be able to use it if needed but he was comforted by its presence in his hand. With each step the horse took, Billy's head drooped a little lower.

"Hold it right there, mister."

Billy lifted his head with effort and squinted, searching the dwelling. Spying the barrel of a rifle sticking out the window, he pulled Rail to a stop.

"Who are you and what are you doing here? My husband will be home in a few minutes so you'd better not try anything."

Billy was listing to the side. "I'm sorry to bother you, ma'am. I'm injured, need help."

"There's a doctor in Boerne and Kendalia. Take your pick. Boerne is closer."

"I would if I could but..." Billy tipped to the side and fell off Rail.

When he awoke, he was lying in a bed. Glancing down, he realized that his shoulder and arm were bandaged.

"Don't move or you'll tear those nice stitches I put in your shoulder."

Billy was mesmerized by the kindness reflected in the woman's eyes. "I thank you for your help." He looked around the one-room home. "How long have I been here?"

"Two days."

"Two..." Billy attempted to sit up only to collapse back onto the bed, closing his eyes and groaning.

"Whoa. It's much too soon for you to get up. A little lower and that bullet would have killed you, Billy."

Billy's eyes shot to hers. "You're mistaking me for someone else. Billy Miner was killed in a shoot-out."

Elizabeth shook her head. "You're Billy Miner." She grinned. "Last year, you and your gang robbed a stagecoach south of Round Rock. I was on that stage returning home after a visit with my sister and her husband. It was quite frightening, I must say, and yet exhilarating to be robbed by the famous Billy Miner. Or should I say infamous?"

She chuckled. "You almost took the necklace I was wearing." She lifted a chain with a gold cross out from beneath the frock she wore. "You told me that I probably needed God's guidance more than you did. Quite cheeky of you, I must say."

Billy's jaw dropped. "I remember that." His eyes roamed her face. "You weren't frightened at all. I'd never robbed anyone who smiled at me."

Elizabeth laughed and held out her hand. "Elizabeth Swanson."

Billy grasped her hand in his. "Pleased to meet you, Elizabeth Swanson."

For the next eight days, Elizabeth nursed Billy back to health. On day five, he could get up and walk outside, albeit slowly. The pain was bearable and he was getting stronger. They talked for hours. He learned that she was a mail-order bride now a widow, having traveled from Boston to Texas. She had an insatiable appetite for details of his escapades, as she called them.

On the morning of the eleventh day, Billy walked out of the cottage and strapped his six-shooter to his hip as Elizabeth returned from the barn. A bandage still covered his shoulder and it was sore, but the stitches were out.

"Your wound needs to finish healing."

"The stitches are out. It's fine." He stared at her. "I can't delay any longer. Ian is going to make his way to the stash west of Austin. That's the only one he knows about, and he'll want to take the loot for himself. I won't let him do that.

"Billy…"

"Lizzy, he betrayed us and Jimmy and Frank are dead because of it. He's gonna pay." He walked back inside to pick up the hat Jimmy had given him.

Elizabeth sighed and walked to the kitchen. She wrapped a loaf of bread and dried meat in a piece of muslin cloth and handed it to him. "Here. This will keep you for a while."

Billy squeezed her arm as he accepted her offering.

She squeezed her hands together. "Will you be coming back this way?" Her hesitant question gave him pause.

Billy set the bread and meat on the table and took her hands in his, staring into her eyes. "I'd like to, if you'll have me."

Her smile lit up the room. "When will you be back?"

"My thieving days are over, Lizzy. But it's long past time that I collect everything and move it all to one location. That will take some time. And I'll have to wait for Ian to show…not sure how long that will take. I figure it will be nigh on two months, maybe more."

For a tough cowboy, the tears gathering in her eyes were nearly his undoing. He reached over and ran his finger down her cheek. "I'll be back, Lizzy, and you won't want for anything. That I promise."

She nodded, sniffing.

Billy donned the hat and they both walked outside. She remained by the door while he saddled Rail. He hoisted himself up into the saddle.

"Be careful Billy."

He half saluted then urged Rail into a trot. He was on a mission and Ian was going to pay.

***

The location of the loot west of Austin was a small cave nestled in an outcropping of rocks at the base of a hill where the river curved. Situated at that juncture were two stones towering more than six feet tall, with a tall cedar tree wedged between them. Oak and cedar trees sparsely lined both sides of the river as it meandered through the rolling hills.

This part of the river was uninhabited, with no roads nearby. From a distance, the location was nondescript.

Up close was a different story. Jimmy had always joked that it was the biggest set of balls and wiener he'd ever seen. The only access to the cave was along the edge of the river, and the entrance was indiscernible. In fact, Billy had discovered it accidentally when Rail threw a shoe and tossed him into the river.

Ian would likely come from Austin so after confirming that the gold and money was still in the cave, Billy hunkered down on the back side of the hill near the top to wait for him.

On the afternoon of the fourth day, the clip clop of horses' hooves drew his attention and he belly crawled to the top to peer over the edge and observe the rider.

It was Ian. He'd recognize that traitor any day of the week. He was alone and looked as though he hadn't a care in the world. Billy seethed, almost drawing his gun and shooting him. But he'd waited this long, a few more minutes wouldn't make a difference.

Billy watched as Ian rode up to the stones and cedar tree before pulling on the reins to stop. Standing up in the stirrups, Ian perused the area. He cocked his head to the side. Evidently satisfied that no one was there, Ian dismounted, removed the saddlebags from his horse, and disappeared around the bend.

When he was sure Ian was in the cave, Billy crept down the hill until he was leaning on the stone nearest Ian's horse. His gun was drawn and hanging by his side.

It wasn't long before Billy detected Ian's approach. He was whistling a tune as he rounded the corner. His face paled when he laid eyes on Billy.

Billy straightened and lifted his gun, pointing it at Ian. "Nice of you to bring my gold out of the cave for me, Ian. I'll be taking it from you now."

"B…B…Billy."

"You look like you've seen a ghost. Surprised I'm still alive?"

Ian shook his head. "Thank God you're alive. Everything happened so quickly when we were ambushed. I lost sight of you and Jimmy. They said you were dead…" His voice trailed off and his head reeled back in sudden understanding. "You switched with Jimmy."

"That's right. Both Jimmy and Frank died because of you. What did the Rangers promise for setting a trap?" Billy growled and stepped toward Ian.

"I'm no traitor, I swear Billy. I never ratted you out." Ian spoke rapidly as sweat dripped from his brow.

Billy stared at Ian. "That's exactly what you did and you're gonna pay for it. Now drop the bags."

Licking his lips, Ian leaned down and set the saddle bags on the ground.

"Now back away and…"

Ian scooped up some dirt and tossed it in Billy's eyes while moving to the side and reaching for his gun.

Grunting and trying to wipe the dirt from his eyes with one hand, Ian fired twice in the direction of the shuffling boots.

Ian dropped his weapon, reaching for his shoulder. He ran to his horse and jumped into the saddle, digging his heels into his horse's sides. Squealing in protest and rearing up, his horse nearly unseated Ian before it bolted.

Billy took aim and fired one more shot. Ian slumped forward as he rode away. Billy re-holstered his gun and collected the saddle bags.

Chapter 22

AFTER THE REVELATIONS ABOUT MICHAEL'S FIRM and Robert Smalley, Kent said he was going to dig a little deeper into their business dealings and would tell her if he discovered anything significant. He was also convinced that she was in even more danger than previously thought. There were too many coincidences and he wasn't going to take any chances.

He'd announced that he'd be staying at Claire's place at night for the foreseeable future. During the day, he'd take care of the case, his ranch business, and the girls after school.

That night, Claire didn't sleep well. Her husband had worked for the development firm owned by Ian Smalley's great-grandson and had met William. How was that possible? Was Robert Smalley aware of William's lineage and, if so, how did he find out? Were they planning to build a subdivision and shops out this way or was there another reason they were so interested in that plot of land? Could the treasure really be somewhere on the ranch?

After tossing and turning for hours, Claire went downstairs, careful not to wake Eddie. Walking into the kitchen, she flipped on the light and made a pot of coffee.

While it was brewing, she headed to the sink and splashed cold water on her face to relieve the grittiness in her eyes.

Bear ambled over from his bed by the fireplace and plopped down by the back door. His soulful look made her chuckle. Pouring herself a cup of coffee, she walked over to Bear, patted him on the head and scratched behind his ears. "Here you go, fella." She opened the back door. "Go do your thing then check on the critters in the barn." He wagged his tail then bounded out of the house without looking back.

Laughing softly, she closed the door and walked to the office. She sat down at the table and lost herself in her work. Despite being tired, she appreciated the quiet. After re-filling her cup and returning to her seat, she leaned back. As she surveyed the room, she appreciated how organized things were now.

Relevant files were in file cabinets on the wall to her right, and she'd shredded all non-essential documents. The old chair that had been blocking the buffet was now positioned in front of the table and a few paintings she found in the attic of various hill country scenes were hanging on two walls. She liked the space.

Her thoughts drifted to William's will. He'd said something that she'd forgotten until now. She retrieved the documents and pulled the will from its folder, flipping to the part where her inheritance was outlined. "Don't forget about that other treasure."

William was sure the treasure existed and that I'd look for it.

She thought back to the conversation she'd had with William the night he died. They were looking at the trunk and he'd showed her the secret compartment.

"Good morning!"

Claire gasped and jumped in her seat as she turned her head toward the office door. Kent was leaning against the door jam holding a cup of coffee in one hand. He was dressed in jeans and a long-sleeve black cowboy shirt and his hair was wet and neatly combed. His feet were bare.

Claire lifted her eyes to his, blushing under his unwavering stare. "What time is it?"

"A little after six. How long have you been up?" He straightened and walked to the chair, settling himself before taking a sip of his coffee.

Claire shrugged. "A few hours. I couldn't sleep." She caught a whiff of his after shave. *Geez, did he have to smell so good?* She was acutely aware of her baggy grey sweatpants, Cal Poly sweatshirt that had seen better days, and tangled hair hanging down her back.

"You're going to wear yourself out."

"Huh? Oh…" She waved that away. "I'm fine. I appreciate the quiet of the mornings before Eddie wakes up and the day begins."

"I get it."

A comfortable silence fell between them, each sipping their coffee.

After a few minutes, Kent sighed then stood. "I need to get to work."

Claire followed suit. "I was going to make breakfast tacos. Do you want a couple?"

He shook his head as they walked out of the office. "I'll take a rain check. Thanks. What are your plans for the day?"

"After I drop Eddie off at school, I'm meeting Grace at the bistro for coffee. Then I'll be back here working. I spoke with Jackie yesterday and she's picking Eddie up from daycare and bringing him home."

"That's nice." He turned toward Eddie's bedroom. "If you deviate from that or your plans change, call me."

"Yes sir." Claire rolled her eyes as she headed to the kitchen.

After a busy half day, Claire made a quick lunch and enjoyed a few moments of serenity on the porch before returning to the office.

She looked down at the table and realized that the will was still there. Re-reading William's comment about the other treasure she thought back to when he showed her the empty compartment. He'd said he put the map in a safe place, a place Billy would appreciate.

What did he mean by that? This house didn't exist back then, and it was doubtful that Billy lived on this land. Even William had given up looking here. Pretty much everything about Boerne had changed since the eighteen hundreds. He never met his great-grandfather, so how would he know what Billy would appreciate?

Claire shot out of her chair and raced to the fireplace. Standing on the hearth, she took down the picture of Billy from over the mantle. She carefully flipped the painting to the backside. Nothing. Leaning the front of the painting against the sofa, she moved her hand down the entire back of the painting to make sure it wasn't hidden inside. It was as smooth as glass. *Seriously?* That was the perfect place to hide it. Grumbling, she returned the picture to the mantle.

Deflated, she walked back to the office. Her eyes fell on Elizabeth's buffet. She rushed over and opened each drawer and the two cabinet doors. All empty. Frowning, she closed the drawers and cabinet doors, then pulled the buffet out from the wall a couple of inches and looked behind it. Nothing was taped to the back. She pulled the buffet further out, then tilted it backward so that the top was resting against the wall. Holding it in place, she knelt down and looked underneath. Still nothing. Discouraged, she eased it back to the ground.

She opened the cabinet doors to further inspect. Placing her hands inside, she moved them over the surface. Nothing. She repeated the process with the two smaller drawers. Nothing. She opened the large drawer and when her fingers touched the back right corner it felt different, softer. Knocking on it, the sound was muffled.

Pulling out the drawer completely, she discovered a slight bulge. Reaching up to the corner, she peeled back the edge of the paper revealing the corner of a brown piece of paper. She peeled it back further until a wrinkled brown piece of paper fell to the bottom of the drawer.

With shaking hands, she picked up the paper and unfolded it. In her hands was a nineteenth century treasure map.

Chapter 23

THAT EVENING, CLAIRE WAS FINISHING DINNER preparations when Kent and Eddie walked in through the back door. "Good timing. Dinner is ready."

Kent accepted a beer from Claire and sat down at the table while Claire settled Eddie in his high chair. "That kid has more energy… My girls were never that full of fire. Does he ever stop?"

Claire smiled. "Only at bedtime. Dig in."

Kent helped himself to a couple pieces of meatloaf, mashed potatoes and gravy, and some green beans. He skipped the salad, offering only "Bunny food" as the reason why.

Claire gave him a mock-scandalized look then served Eddie and herself. "Any news about the case or the stolen trunk?" She refused to ask how his day went. That felt too much like something a wife would ask her husband.

He shook his head. "Ethan walked the sides of the property near the front wall with Ben, but they didn't find any breaches in the fence. Ben also rode along the entire perimeter. The fence was intact."

Claire frowned.

"It had to be someone with access." He paused. "You gave me a new gate code. Does that mean you canceled all gate codes and created new ones?" Claire nodded. "Who got the new codes?"

"Ben, Jill, Clyde, Erwin, you, and me. The Sheriff's office and Fire Department have master codes, of course, in case of emergency. That's six total. Everyone else has to call at the entrance. I also created a list with everyone who now has access along with their assigned code. It's on the computer."

"Good. Who had the codes before?"

"No clue. But I deleted ten codes." She took a bite of mashed potatoes before offering a bite to Eddie.

"So there are three or four unaccounted people who had codes."

She shrugged. "I had a code. Maybe the others were unused." She paused, a fork of meatloaf halfway to her mouth. "Actually, Jackie probably had a code as well given how she helped William. I told you about the meal she brought over the night I had dinner with him."

"That's right. You said it was a little awkward."

Claire nodded. "That's putting it mildly. I could have picked it up myself and saved Jackie the trip, but William said she liked to help. Jackie agreed but..."

"What else could she do?"

"Exactly."

After dinner and once Eddie was in bed, Claire went into the office and returned to the living room where Kent was relaxing with some coffee. She handed him the map and sank into the couch next to him.

"What's this?" He unfolded the paper then looked up at Claire.

"I found it this afternoon in the buffet." She told him how she figured it out. "I was bursting to tell you earlier but Jackie was dropping off Eddie, and then between dinner and putting Eddie to bed…"

He whistled in appreciation. "It certainly looks old enough. I can have our forensic team take a look and tell us the age. Have you looked at it?"

"No, I had just found it when you arrived." Scooting closer to him, they both studied it. "William wasn't kidding when he said it was a crude map."

At the top of the page was the first X. From there, a dashed line went straight down the page with a second dashed line breaking off to the right. At the juncture where the two dashed lines split was a drawing of what looked like a well on one side and two conjoined trees or bushes on the other. Further down was a second X by two parallel lines that had dashes crossing them at regular intervals. A smudge of dirt or something partially obscured it.

What looked like three buildings were located at various points along the dashed line that had split to the right. One had multiple circles inside, the word *Inn* was written inside another, and the third building that was furthest away looked like a church. A squiggly line ran across the map just above the church. The last X was below the building marked *Inn*. Water spots in a couple of places blurred portions of the map.

"Where is this? Is this even in Boerne?" Kent flipped the paper over to check the backside. "No town name is written anywhere."

"And I count three Xs. Is one of them the location of the treasure or is it spread among all three?"

Kent blew out his breath. "The dashed lines could be roads but there's no legend and no compass. Are we even holding the map the right way?"

"I'm not surprised William gave up. You could go crazy trying to figure it out." She excused herself to check on Eddie.

Kent nodded and folded the map.

When Claire returned, Kent was in the kitchen putting the map in a Ziplock bag. "I don't want it damaged when I take it in tomorrow."

"I don't want your forensic team to look at it, Kent. Right now, you and I are the only two people who are aware that it exists. I want to keep it that way. Good idea to put it in a Ziplock though, thanks."

"Put the map someplace safe."

"I will." She leaned her hip against the island. "Is there any news about Lenny?"

"He was shot with a twenty-two caliber pistol on the far side of the square. A witness who was out for a morning walk remembered seeing him walk from the Cibolo Creek Trail toward the Square. She was on the opposite corner heading toward Main Street and had stopped to tie her shoe when she noticed someone in jeans walking toward him. A van rounding the corner blocked her view but when it passed by Lenny was holding his chest and running across the Square, probably heading to you. The other person was gone."

"What? That's a good quarter mile from my office. Oh my gosh. Poor Lenny."

"She couldn't give any details about the person in jeans. She wasn't even sure if it was a man or a woman. The person caught her attention because of a red beanie cap. She thought it odd that someone would wear a bean-ie cap when it wasn't cold outside." He paused. "We also got results on the DNA testing. The cigarettes found on your property were his."

"Why would Lenny follow me?"

Kent shook his head. "There could be any number of reasons, infatuation or a fixation of some sort. We ran a background check. You knew he was in the military. That was about a decade ago, after serving two tours in Iraq. He could have continued to serve, but opted for the medical discharge they offered after learning that his wife was pregnant. A month after returning home to San Antonio, his wife and unborn son were killed in a robbery outside of Walmart."

"He told me he was married and his wife and child had died, but he didn't give any details. How awful! Wait, what was her name?"

"His wife? Evelyn."

They exchanged a glance. "Evie." They said her name simultaneously.

"He must have been thinking of her right before he died." Claire pushed a stray hair out of her face.

"He took their murders hard. Between that and his experiences in Iraq, he lost it and his parents checked him into a facility to help him deal with his PTSD. Two years later, he moved to Boerne. He's been here ever since. Kept to himself, no known friends. His address was a post office box. We're not sure where he lived." He studied Claire. "He was a soldier. I'd be willing to bet that he felt protective toward you since you're a single mom and he couldn't protect or save his own wife and child."

Claire wiped a tear off her cheek. "That is unbeliev-ably sad. The poor man." She looked at Kent. "He died because he was watching over me?" Closing her eyes, she took a deep breath in then blew it out. She opened her eyes when Kent reached over and grabbed her hand.

"In other news, we released your office this afternoon. Officially, it's no longer a crime scene and you can go back anytime."

Claire scrunched her nose and shook her head. "I spoke with the owner when I was moving out of the apartment and gave my notice for the office as well. It didn't make sense to use one space but not the other. He gave me forty-five days to clear out. I'll inform him tomorrow that I'll be out of the space before Thanksgiving."

"Are you okay?" Still holding her hand, he squeezed.

A spark ran from their hands to her chest. Claire took a quick breath, her gaze colliding with Kent's. She licked her lips. "Kent…"

He released her hand and ran his finger from her cheek to her lips. "Claire, why aren't we together when there is obviously still something between us?"

She looked away from the hurt reflected in his eyes. "I…I…I told you a bit about my marriage. What I didn't tell you is that, unknown to me, he'd maxed out a high-end, high-limit credit card, a card I didn't even want him to get. And he'd just purchased his truck the year before. He told me he paid cash for it, but I found out after he died that it was financed through a credit union that we had no previous business with. I didn't know anything about our financial status, and my expertise is finance, for crying out loud. I had a baby on the way and I couldn't pay my bills."

She shifted and raised her eyes to his.

"Fortunately, my aunt helped me. She told me to sell the house, which I did, and move in with her. She was a godsend. I paid off his debts when the house sold. And she helped with Eddie while I built up my business. In the two years that I lived with her, I was able to build up a small nest egg. When we moved here, I figured I'd be able to buy a modest house for us in about two years. I vowed never to let myself give up control of things and never be dependent on someone else. I will never be in that situation again."

"That explains a lot. You amaze me." She didn't miss the admiration in his voice. "You endured a terrible tragedy and still managed to create an incredible life for you and Eddie. You're the strongest woman I know. Thank you for sharing, but your reasoning is flawed for one main reason." He pinned her with his stare. "I'm not Michael. I would never try to control you, and I've always believed that marriage is a partnership. Sharing everything is part of that."

He chuckled in a self-deprecating way. "Truth be told, that's why Sheila left us. She wasn't interested in a partnership. She would go out with her friends two or three times a week, even after the girls were born, and didn't share anything. I knew she had secrets and that she wasn't happy, but I couldn't fix it and, quite honestly, I was too busy with work and taking care of the girls. Sheila finally left saying she was more interested in life in a large city than the ranching life."

Kent paused and looked down for a moment. "She also informed me that she'd been involved in a long-term affair with a married man and that the girls might not be mine."

Claire gasped. "I'm so sorry, Kent."

"Water under the bridge at this point. The girls were mine whether DNA proved it or not. I checked though because I didn't want Sheila to be able to lay claim to them later. Louise is my biological daughter, Ginger is not. To protect them, I forced her to sign away all rights to the girls in the divorce."

He grasped her hand and squeezed. "Marriage should be and can be a beautiful expression of love between two people who are right for each other. Life is too short to walk away from the possibility of that, don't you agree?" He smiled. "Now don't panic. I'm not suggesting marriage…well, not right away." He winked at her. "Give us a chance. We might discover something truly beautiful."

Tears formed in Claire's eyes as she nodded. Sniffing, she said, "I can do that."

Kent's face lit up with his grin. He leaned over and kissed her gently on the mouth. "Good." He rose from the couch. "One more thing, plan on putting your cowboy boots on because I've already spoken with Ethan, and the four of us are going to Luckenbach this Friday. We need a break from everything that's going on."

"I'm in."

"Okay, on that note, I'm going to say goodnight. I have an early appointment tomorrow." He pointed his finger at her. "Don't forget to put the map someplace safe and text me your schedule."

Claire chuckled and lightly punched him in the arm. "You're still an ass." She turned and walked toward her bedroom, grinning the whole way. "Good night, Kent."

Chapter 24

THE NEXT MORNING, KENT ARRIVED AT the office early to follow up with his contact in Dallas. He'd just picked up the phone to dial when there was a rap on his door.

"Got a minute?" Jeremy Hanson poked his head into Kent's office.

Setting the phone down, Kent waved him in. "How's Pablo Gonzalez?"

"He's a cool dude." Jeremy sat down in the chair opposite Kent. "This temporary duty isn't what I was expecting."

Kent grinned. "Mixing with the rich and famous isn't your thing?"

"Oh, it's definitely my thing but the whining wives and girlfriends are not." Jeremy chuckled. "My last day is the day after tomorrow and our services are not needed at the wedding on Saturday." He cleared his throat, glancing down at his hands. When he looked up, Kent observed for the first time uncertainty in his eyes. "I'd like to be put back on the Miner murder case."

"A client of Claire's was murdered three days ago…"

Jeremy nodded. "In her office, right?"

"He wasn't murdered in her office but he made it there, after he was shot. He evidently wanted to tell her something."

"What did he tell her?"

"That he was at William Miner's ranch the night he was killed."

Jeremy leaned forward. "So he killed Miner?"

Kent shook his head. "He was out front, saw a flash inside and then observed someone walking out the front door. He thought the killer heard him. Evidently, he was right. Unfortunately, Lenny wasn't able to identify him."

Jeremy leaned back and whistled before fixing Kent with his stare. "I can see that this is a complex case. I want back on it."

"Because of the murder in town, Ethan is now working the case with me." Kent reached for a piece of paper on the side of his desk. "A new case came in two days ago involving the theft of jewelry in Tapatio Springs. Deputy Smith began preliminaries yesterday. It's not a murder, but it's an excellent opportunity for you to get more acclimated to solving cases. You can work with her again. This is a brief summary, Deputy Smith has the case file. I was actually going to reach out to you later today." He held the paper out toward Jeremy.

After a slight hesitation, Jeremy took it from Kent's hand. Shoulders sagging, he looked down with a slight frown on his face. Sighing deeply, Jeremy looked up. "I owe you an apology for my behavior and attitude before my temporary assignment." He scratched his forehead. "I was eager to get the chance to work on a murder case and I overstepped and came off as a boor. For that I apologize."

He glanced back down at the paper before raising his eyes to Kent again. "Of course I'll work on this case with Deputy Smith but it's a cake walk and won't take up every minute of my day. I can learn much more from you and Miner's murder. Is there any way I can assist when I'm not working on this theft? I'll work weekends and nights if needed."

Kent sat back in his chair as he considered Jeremy's request. He didn't completely buy the contrite attitude or the attempt to butter him up. But he could certainly use his help, have him assist with research and security as needed. And he did need Jeremy to get up to speed on the nuances of the job if he was going to remain in the department. Leaning forward, he placed his elbows on the desk.

"Here's the deal. You can assist on the Miner case as long as it doesn't interfere with this other case. It has priority. There are research and security opportunities, however, where your assistance would be helpful."

Jeremy let out a breath and stood, offering his hand to Kent. "I appreciate this opportunity and will do my best to prove to you that I can do the job."

Kent stood and reached over the desk to shake his hand. "Get with Deputy Smith and then reach out to me tomorrow and I'll have some tasks for you."

"Thank you, Lieutenant. I appreciate this and won't let you down."

Jeremy turned and walked to the door.

"Oh, and Jeremy?" Hand on the doorknob, Jeremy looked over his shoulder. "You owe an apology to Mrs. St. John the next time you see her."

Jeremy nodded then opened the door and walked out.

Kent watched Jeremy depart, a thoughtful look on his face. Returning to his seat, he was reaching for his phone when it rang.

"Lieutenant Adams."

"Kent, it's Ethan. I just got back from watching Lenny Crater's autopsy. The bullet is a match to the one that killed William Miner."

Chapter 25

THE WEEK PASSED BY UNEVENTFULLY FOR Claire.

She planned to keep her existing clients but not accepting any new ones, and she conducted zoom meetings with all of them to explain how things were changing. Most were okay with the changes, a couple of local clients said they preferred to meet with someone in person, so Claire gave them the names of two local advisors that they might consider using and they parted ways amicably.

She met with Grace to discuss changes to her website, including simplifying some things that an authenticated user could do once logged in. Since she was not growing her business, there was no need for some of the more complex functionality, like having an auto-generated budgeting tool. She still planned to offer guidance on budgeting but wanted an online manual with exercises instead so users could learn how to budget. She was convinced that learning how to budget would be more beneficial for them.

Claire went on another tour of the property with Ben, and learned about the wells and septic systems as they rode through the pastures and to the stock tank. She appreciated Ben's knowledge and was eager to explore some more soon, even planning to bring Eddie with her the next time.

She and Kent slid into a routine as well, enjoying dinner each evening, playing with Eddie, and discovering more about each other. By mutual agreement, they didn't talk about the case and where things stood. Kent would provide her with relevant information when warranted, and she didn't want to bother him with unnecessary questions. He did mention that Deputy Hanson would provide minimal assistance again beginning next week. She didn't like that idea but it wasn't her decision so she didn't complain.

She wasn't idle where William's murder and the case were concerned.

She pulled out the map every day to study it, often bringing up different hill country towns—from Comfort, Boerne and Blanco to Round Rock, Austin and Fredericksburg—on the computer to try to gauge if any town looked like it could possibly be the town in the map. She compared each town from every angle of the map, all to no avail. There were just too many changes in the past one hundred plus years.

On the Friday before Thanksgiving, Claire kept Eddie out of school. As the temperatures were still quite warm, she dressed him in a pair of shorts and a T-shirt with 'I'm Mommy's Angel' blazoned across the front. After breakfast, they both headed outside for some fresh air. Eddie took off toward the barn, Bear right by his side, with Claire following more slowly.

Jill was walking out of the barn as Claire approached. "Good morning Claire." Dressed in a white blouse, blue skirt with matching blazer, she looked like she was headed to an interview, minus the tennis shoes.

Claire took in the whole picture, giggling when her eyes fell on the shoes. "And a good morning to you. I can't tell if you're going to an appointment or for a run."

"An interview actually. The bank on Main Street is hiring for a part-time position as a teller. With Sarah growing up and needing less of my time, it's a good time for me to get out of the house." She grinned. "My heels are in the car. I just came to tell Ben I was heading out."

"That's a great idea, Jill. Good luck."

"Thanks." She turned to walk away then stopped and turned back to Claire. "Listen, I'm picking Sarah up from school this afternoon and taking her out for an ice cream and to the park. Why don't I take Eddie with me?"

"He'd love that."

"I'll leave here about a quarter to three."

Claire nodded. "I just need him back by five. Kent is picking us up and we're taking him to Ethan and Grace's. Jo and Chase are looking after the kids and the four of us are going to Luckenbach."

"That sounds like fun! No problem getting him home by then."

"Thanks, Jill."

Claire walked into the barn to speak with Ben then she rounded up Eddie and returned to the house.

At two-forty-five Jill picked up Eddie, who had been bouncing up and down nonstop since Claire told him about his outing. She decided to get ready early. She hadn't danced in years, loved the two-step, and couldn't wait to go to Luckenbach. Kent was right. They needed this break.

Splurging on a long soak in the tub that she sprinkled with lavender, she took her time getting ready, a luxury she didn't often have. After her bath, she applied minimal mascara and a little blush, then braided her hair, opting to leave it hanging down her back. She donned brown jeans and a long-sleeve sunset-orange cotton blouse then sat down on the bed to pull on her boots. Grabbing her cowboy hat, she walked into the kitchen humming a George Strait song.

Claire had just stepped out back and was petting Bear when Kent rounded the corner with blue and red lights flashing on his truck and dust flying behind him. The sirens weren't on but she was still startled and jumped back. He skidded to a stop. Jill's car rounded the corner at a more sedate pace and a police car followed, lights flashing.

Kent jumped out of the truck and rushed up to Claire. "Are you all right? Why haven't you answered your phone? I've called multiple times."

Claire's eyes were wide and her hand was on her chest. "You scared the crap out of me. I'm fine. And I didn't answer the phone because I turned it off so I could enjoy a leisurely bath. The silence was nice so I didn't turn it back on." Her eyes slid to Jill's car and she realized that Ethan was driving. Jill was sitting in the passenger seat crying. Chills ran down her spine. "Where's Eddie?" She choked out past the fear that had lodged in her throat. She pushed Kent to the side and ran to the car.

At the sound of the vehicles, Ben had raced over and was pulling Jill out of the car. He wrapped her in a bear hug then set her aside to open the rear passenger door for Sarah, who was huddled in her seat and sniffling.

Ethan was out of the car and put his hands on Claire's upper arms stopping her. "Eddie is fine. He's in the back. He's a little scared because he doesn't know what's going on."

"That makes two of us." Breathing heavily, she opened the passenger door as Ethan went to the other side of the car to speak with Ben. A moment later, Ben left with Jill and Sarah to walk the short distance to their house, Sarah in his arms and Jill leaning heavily on him.

"Mama, Mama, Mama." Eddie was sniffling and crocodile tears were rolling down his cheeks as he held his arms out.

Claire leaned in and hugged him, breathing in his little boy scent and fighting off tears for unknown reasons. She leaned back and unbuckled him from his car seat. "You've had quite the adventure, haven't you?" Pulling him out of the seat and car, she turned him so he could see the police car. "Did you like the flashing lights? My goodness, and here I thought you were just going to have some ice cream." She tried to make light of things as she bounced him on her hip.

He took his thumb out of his mouth and pointed at the lights. "Blue. Red."

"Yes, Sweetie. Good job with your colors." She walked past Ethan and Kent and into the house, taking Eddie into her bedroom. Bear followed her inside.

Twenty minutes later, she joined Kent and Ethan in the living room sitting down on the sofa next to Kent. "I managed to get him to sleep. He's snuggling with Bear." She glared at both men. "You scared my son and I half out of our wits. What the hell is going on? And why was Jill crying?"

Kent took her hand in his. "I'm sorry…I thought… something might have happened to you."

He glanced at Ethan who pulled out a baggie with a piece of paper inside. "Claire, while Jill was at the park with Sarah and Eddie, she briefly turned her attention to Sarah who had fallen down. When she looked behind her for Eddie, he was gone."

"Oh my God." Claire paled.

"He wasn't far," Kent assured her. "He was sitting on a bench on the other side of the playground eating a piece of chocolate."

Claire's rubbed her temple, confusion written on her face. "Chocolate? They were going to have ice cream."

"They had ice cream before they went to the park." Eddie handed her the baggie. "Jill found this note tucked into the waistband of his shorts."

Claire read the note as tears welled up in her eyes. The baggie with the note fell to the ground.

Scribbled on a wrapper were the words: "Don't take what belongs to me or I will take what belongs to you."

Chapter 26

ETHAN LEFT THE TWO ALONE so Claire could gather herself, returning a few minutes later with two sodas and a glass of wine. Pushing away from Kent, she accepted the wine with a nod of thanks. He handed the soda to Kent and all three drank in silence for a couple of minutes.

"I called Grace and informed her of the situation and that Luckenbach is obviously out for tonight. She sends her love and said she'll call you tomorrow to talk."

"Thanks, Ethan." She set the glass on the coffee table. "How would anyone know where Eddie was going to be? Jill and I spoke just this morning about Eddie going with her."

Kent shook his head. "We don't know. The officer who followed us swept the house in case it was bugged, all except your bedroom while you were with Eddie, just to be sure. It's all clear. Someone could be watching the property and keeping track of comings and goings."

Ethan nodded. "It's also possible that it was just a fluke, a random opportunity that he or she didn't want to pass up." He reached down and picked up the baggie with the note. "This looks like a sandwich wrapper with the words scribbled on it as if done in haste. Perhaps someone in town was eating lunch and saw Eddie with Jill and Sarah at the ice cream shop and followed them to the park. We're canvasing the restaurants in the area to determine who uses this type of wrapper."

Kent added, "Forensics will test it for prints and they may be able to give us more info about the wrapper that could help, type of food that was eaten, that sort of thing."

"There is one other possibility." Claire hesitated. "Jill and/or Ben could be involved. I hate to say it and I don't really believe it but…"

Kent pressed his lips together and clasped his hands together. "We've considered that, Claire, and we're pursuing that avenue as well."

Claire sighed.

"I'm wondering why anyone would even go after Eddie and why now." Ethan looked at Claire. "The trunk was stolen, there is no map, and most people in town don't even believe that William is Billy Miner's great-grandson."

Claire's eyes slid to Kent. His eyebrow was raised as he stared at her. Sighing, she stood and walked over to the refrigerator. Opening the freezer drawer, she reached inside and shifted meat, peas, and frozen waffles out of the way before pulling out a Ziplock bag. She returned to the living room and silently handed it to Ethan, sitting down next to Kent once more.

Kent leaned close, whispering, "The freezer? When I told you to put it someplace safe, that isn't exactly what I had in mind."

"That's where I used to put credit cards I didn't want to use anymore. I figured that not many people would think to look there." Claire winked at him.

Ethan's eyes were wide. "This is what I'm thinking it is, right?"

Fixing her gaze on him, Claire straightened and nodded. "Only you, Kent and I know of its existence."

He gazed at the map. "Where did you find it?" Claire spent the next ten minutes explaining her rationale for looking where she did and how she ultimately found it. Ethan whistled. "Boy, William was one wily dude. I'm impressed." He turned the map in different angles. "Which way is north?"

Kent shrugged. "We assume in the direction where the words are right side up but they could have been added later. We can't even tell what town this is."

"Although I've been thinking…" Claire began.

"Hold on to your hat, she's thinking." Kent smiled and winked at her.

Ethan chuckled.

"Ha ha ha." She scrunched her nose. "I'm going to look for maps from the eighteen-hundreds of a few hill country towns and compare them to Billy's map. If I can identify any markers, I might be able to pinpoint the correct town. I'm not sure I can find historical maps with that level of detail, but it's worth a try."

"Good." Kent glanced at Ethan before continuing. "Now we need to talk about your safety, both you and Eddie." He studied Claire as he spoke.

Claire held up a hand. "I've already decided to take Eddie to my aunt's place in San Antonio. She travels to Kentucky every year to spend Thanksgiving with her sister. I'm sure she'd love to take Eddie with her. I'm calling her tonight and I plan to drive him to San Antonio in the morning. My hope is that she'll fly to Lexington tomorrow." She titled her chin up as she watched Kent. "But I'm staying here."

"Bullshit. It's too dangerous." Kent's reaction was immediate.

"I'm not running away, Kent." She narrowed her eyes. "But I'm also not going to put my son at risk. While I'm disappointed that I won't be with him at Thanksgiving, he'll have fun with Aunt Jen and I'll be able to focus on figuring out what's going on and finding the treasure."

Both men began to speak, but she put her hands up.

"I won't get in the way of your investigation, but neither am I going to sit idly by and wait for someone to come after me." Crossing her arms, she stared at Kent. "Maybe I'll even be able to assist you in some way."

Kent rubbed his forehead and looked at Ethan, who was grinning. "See what I have to deal with?"

"Claire and Grace are two peas in a pod. Welcome to my world." Ethan stood. "On that note, I need to get out of here. Officer Jenkins is driving me back to my car in town." He turned to Claire. "Be safe and do what Kent tells you to do." Her eyebrow shot up. Ethan shook his head. "At least be safe."

She chuckled. "And I will do what Kent tells me to do, promise." Her face lost its humor as she hugged Ethan. "Thank you for today."

He nodded. "I told Ben that I want to speak with Jill again tomorrow so I'll be back." Claire nodded and he turned to go.

Kent walked Ethan out as Claire walked into the kitchen to figure out what to eat for dinner. When he returned, he joined Claire in the kitchen leaning his hip against the island. "I'm going with you to San Antonio tomorrow. Ethan is renting a car tonight for us and we'll meet him in Leon Springs on the way. Don't tell anyone what we're doing, not even Ben."

Claire nodded. "Okay." She walked over to Kent, stopping when she stood in front of him. Stretching up on her toes, she pulled his head down for a kiss. "Thank you, for everything. I don't know what I'd do if…"

"Nothing is going to happen to Eddie. I won't let it." Kent enveloped her in a hug.

Chapter 27

EARLY SATURDAY MORNING, KENT DROVE CLAIRE and Eddie to San Antonio. If the situation wasn't so serious, Claire would giggle in delight at the subterfuge and clandestine mood. They left at dawn, light enough but with headlights still needed. Kent said he wanted to keep an eye out for anyone who might follow them.

As soon as Kent pulled out of the ranch, Eddie had fallen back asleep. Shifting in her seat so she could observe him, her heart swelled with love. Still wearing his Spiderman pajamas, his head lolled to the side of his car seat and his stuffed puppy was about to slip out of his lax arms. His curly hair fell across his forehead as he softly snored. Claire sent a prayer of thanks to God for giving her such a sweet son.

On full alert, Kent didn't speak much as he drove through town toward interstate ten. He stayed off the main roads as he made his way to the interstate. When they pulled into the HEB parking lot, Ethan was waiting for them. Ethan would take Kent's truck to his ranch and they'd swap vehicles later in the afternoon. After moving their stuff into the rental car, they continued to San Antonio.

Eddie was excited to see Aunt Jen, a feeling that Jen reciprocated, and Claire was grateful that Eddie didn't fuss when they said their goodbyes. Her aunt was over-the-moon of having an open-ended stay with her sister and her favorite great-nephew and told Claire not to worry about a thing. A weight lifted off Claire's shoulders as they disappeared inside the airport. She closed her eyes, relishing the lightness. When she opened them, Kent was staring at her and smiling.

"You look relieved."

"I am. Knowing he'll be safe a few states away eases my mind on so many levels." Claire turned teary eyes to him. "I'm still going to miss him, though."

"It won't be the same without him here." He touched her cheek with his finger. "But we'll figure out what's going on and get him home as soon as possible."

Shooting Kent a sly look, Claire rubbed her hands together. "Time to get to work."

When Kent and Claire arrived at Ethan's later that morning, they were greeted with noisy chaos. The coffee table in the living room had been pushed aside and Jo, Chase, Ginger, and Louise were playing a boisterous game of Twister. Louise was laughing as she tried to hold her position without falling, but as soon as she spied her dad, she collapsed with a strangled "Dad!"

Ginger squealed and raced to him arriving before Louise since she was lying under Jo who was laughing outright. "I'm so glad you're here," she exclaimed as she launched herself into his arms.

Kent laughed and twirled her around, giving her a loud kiss on her forehead. "It's only been two days, squirt."

"I still missed you." She grabbed his ears and yanked him toward her so she could give a loud smacking kiss of her own.

Setting Ginger down, he wrapped Louise in a bear hug and asked if she was being a polite guest.

Before she could answer, Grace walked into the room. "Your daughters are the best guests ever, and we're glad they're here. We may not give them back."

Grace pulled Claire's arm through hers and they walked toward the kitchen. "How did things go with Eddie and your aunt? Have you two eaten? It's still early. The kids ate, but I was just getting ready to cook for Ethan and I."

Claire's stomach chose that moment to grumble. She looked at Grace and both women laughed.

"I guess I have my answer. Sit down while I pull out a few more eggs."

"I can't hide anything when I'm hungry."

The men joined the women and conversation flowed while the food was prepared and eaten. Afterward, the men excused themselves to talk about the case while Grace and Claire cleaned up.

"How are you doing?" Grace paused wiping the counter as she studied Claire.

"So much better now that Eddie is safe." Claire sighed. "And determined."

Grace patted Claire's hand. "Ethan told me what happened at the park. That must have been so scary."

"Terrifying. You went through something similar with Jo just a few months ago. How did you cope?"

"One day at a time surrounded by people I love and who love me...and a lot of prayer."

Stepping over to Grace, Claire gave her a quick hug then returned to the dishes in the sink. "Thanks, Grace."

"Anytime hon." Grace dropped the towel over the oven rail. "Now, let's forget about the rest of these dishes because I want to talk to you about a few things."

Claire set the plate down and turned toward Grace. "This sounds serious."

Grace avoided Claire's eyes as she turned toward the back door. "Let's step outside." Claire followed, pulling the door shut behind her.

Taking a deep breath, Grace turned and faced Claire. "I'm a little hesitant to bring this up." She grimaced. "Ethan told me about the map. Your secret is safe with me," she rushed to add. "The only reason I brought it up is because there's a program where you can place one map on top of another. You can turn both maps whichever way you want, and you can do things like age trees and stretch a street for a better fit. It's a pretty cool program. I incorporated it into a project that I did for a client last year." She trailed off as she wrung her hands and waited.

"Wow! This is going to make it so much easier to try to figure the map out. Thank you so much!"

Grace's shoulders sagged. "I was worried that you'd be angry that Ethan told me."

"Are you kidding? I'm ecstatic." She paused. "Although I am concerned because William and Lenny were likely killed because of the treasure and this map."

"You don't have to worry. I won't mention it to anyone and we won't discuss it here." She reached into her pocket and pulled out a flash drive. "This is for you."

Claire took the flash drive, eager to try out the program. "So what's the other thing you wanted to discuss?"

Grace smiled. "Absent my father, Jo is going to walk me down the aisle."

"I love that! Although I guess I assumed she was going to be your maid of honor."

"No, I was saving that for you."

"What? Really?"

Grace grasped Claire's hands in hers. "Positive, and Jo was thrilled when I told her what I wanted to do."

"This is such an honor." They hugged before going back inside.

Chapter 28

By early afternoon, Claire was ready to go home and dive into the program Grace had given her. Ethan followed them because he planned to speak with Jill again.

Before going to the office, she walked with Ethan and Kent to Ben and Jill's house. She wanted to check on Jill, make sure she was okay.

Jill opened the door, her lips quivering. "Claire, I'm so sorry."

Claire hugged her. "It wasn't your fault. Getting distracted could happen to anyone. How's Sarah?"

Jill shook her head as she pulled away. "Thank you for asking about Sarah. She's fine, tripped on a root and scraped her knee." She turned toward Ethan and Kent. "I've been expecting you. Come on in." She opened the door wider.

Claire excused herself and returned to the main house. She walked straight to the freezer and pulled the map out of the drawer. Carefully removing it from the Ziplock bag, she snapped a picture from her camera then returned it to its hiding place. Moving to the office, she inserted the flash drive into the computer and opened the program Grace gave her.

She searched online for maps of Boerne, Austin, and Round Rock. Given how much time Billy spent in those locations, she figured that they were the most likely places for him to hide the treasure. If nothing panned out, she'd move on to Comfort, Johnson City, and Fredericksburg. She then uploaded the picture of the treasure map into the program.

Boerne was the logical first choice since Billy was ambushed in town and William lived there.

Claire opened up the Boerne map. There were only two sides of the treasure map that realistically looked like it could be the correct orientation. Starting with the wide, or landscape, side, she positioned the treasure map on top of the city map.

Realizing that the treasure map was too big compared to the city map, she shrunk the size of the map image. Then she shifted the treasure map from side to side and up and down to see if it 'fit' the city map. She also tried stretching the landmarks within the treasure map since the likelihood that it was drawn to scale was slim. She played with it for about an hour, but it became apparent that this side wasn't the correct orientation.

She reset the treasure map then flipped it ninety degrees to the portrait side and tried again. Once more, she had to shrink the map image. She shifted the map to the right and two streets appeared to line up with the dashed lines on the treasure map. Assuming that the straight dashed line was Old School Road, then the other dashed line to the right had to be Main Street. It didn't line up perfectly, but it was close. After lining up the two streets, she stretched the bottom half of landmarks within the treasure map so that the squiggly line matched the

Boerne River on the city map and the church matched the Catholic church further south. Her heart thumped and her hands were shaking.

But when she looked at the top part of the treasure map and compared it to the city map, there were no railroad tracks on that side of town. She also knew that where the two roads split, an empty lot was on the right side and a gas station was on the left. She stretched and tweaked it anyway until it fit as good as possible.

Understanding that things change, and there certainly was no gas station in the eighteen hundreds, she wrote off the two landmarks on the treasure map where the road split as progress over time.

The railroad track was now crossing Johns Road and ran parallel to Old School Road. The 'X' next to it on the treasure map was the middle school today. She'd have to research what was there in the eighteen hundreds, but even if it was a smaller school, she couldn't imagine treasure being there. Besides, the building was obviously torn down at some point to build the current school.

Claire was somewhat reassured when the inn on the treasure map matched the inn that sat next to the plaza. And the building on Billy's map that had circles inside was probably a bank. There were other buildings next to it now, and even back then, but she was fairly certain that the circles most likely represented coins as they were still used for payment back then. Not only that, Billy Miner had tried to rob the bank the day he was ambushed, so assuming it was a bank made the most sense to her.

Stretching her arms above her head, she leaned back then rolled her head from side to side, shrieking when a hand landed on her shoulder.

Chapter 29

She twisted in the chair. "Don't sneak up on me like that!"

Kent grinned sheepishly. "Sorry. You were so intent on what you were doing, I didn't want to interrupt you until you took a break."

Claire shook her head. "My heart will drop back down from my throat in a minute."

Kent leaned down so he could look at the monitor. "How's it going?"

"Um, good I think." She explained what she'd done so far. "…but there are no tracks on that side of town and the X's don't seem to point to anything concrete. I can't tell if the X by the inn is supposed to be in front of it or inside. The hotel has been there since the eighteen-fifties, so the treasure could be there. Although if there's as much treasure as people say, it would have been found."

He frowned. "There are a lot of years between then and now. So much has changed, even the topography."

"Well, this is just the first town. Maybe there will be a better match with Austin or Round Rock."

"It can wait. I'm starving. I'm taking you out to dinner." He kissed her neck then straightened.

Claire was grinning as she saved her work onto the flash drive then pulled it out and put it in her pocket. "Is that so?" She shut down the computer and closed the monitor.

Pulling her out of the chair, they walked out of the office. "Yep, I'm going to wine and dine you. I even made a reservation." He wiggled his eyebrows up and down. Claire burst out laughing.

On the drive to town, Claire's breath caught at how handsome he was. More importantly, he was optimistic and had an easy way about him.

Kent parked across the street from the Oak Grill, an upscale and elegant restaurant downtown.

"Ooh la la, so fancy." She placed her hand on his arm as he escorted her across the street.

"Only the best."

It was Saturday evening and the place was packed. The din was loud with laughter, boisterous conversation, and silverware clinking on plates but it didn't detract from the ambiance. Soft lighting and classical music gave the room a comfortable and cozy feel that Claire appreciated as they followed the hostess to their table. She groaned when she smelled steak and spied lobster on someone's table. A few people called out to Kent. He acknowledged them but stayed by her side. Settling in at a table in the rear next to the empty fireplace, Claire sighed.

"Happy?" Kent intertwined their hands.

"Very, despite all that's going on." She squeezed his hand. "Thank you."

They enjoyed a nice bottle of Pinot Noir and devoured juicy steaks, while taking more about their lives before they met. Claire couldn't remember ever connecting with someone so well. It was as if they were in their own world. The conversations she and Michael used to have were more superficial, even in the early stages of their romance and marriage. Only now did she realize how much true intimacy she'd been missing in her marriage.

All too soon, dinner was over and they walked arm in arm to the truck. It was a quiet drive home, but it was a companionable silence as they held hands.

As they approached the back door, Kent stopped when there was a crunch underfoot. Glass glittered. One pane in the window was broken.

He pulled Claire to the side, motioning for her to be quiet and to stay where she was. He quickly returned to the truck to retrieve his gun then approached the door.

"Damn." Kent flipped on the light switch.

Claire tip-toed in behind him. "Oh my God!" Everywhere Claire looked was a disaster. The place had been ransacked. Kent swore again and shoved Claire behind him motioning for her to be quiet.

"Stay put," he whispered and crept forward, but Claire held on to his waist and followed. Stopping, he looked over his shoulder.

"I'm not staying here alone."

After a brief pause, he continued, telling her to stay behind him and do what he said. He walked into the living room where slashed cushions lay on the sofa, the once-neatly stacked logs were scattered all over the room, even the painting of Billy Miner was on the ground. There didn't appear to be any damage to the painting, although the frame probably wasn't salvageable considering all the knife cuts.

Thank God Eddie is in Kentucky.

The back rooms and bathrooms suffered the same fate although the guest bedroom with all the boxes was minimally damaged. Most boxes had not even been opened. Whoever did this was either in a rush and didn't have time to go through everything or they felt that what they were looking for would not be there.

She gasped when Kent turned on the light in the office. Her organized, beautiful space was no more. The contents of the file cabinets were strewn across the room. Papers were everywhere. Her laptop was gone.

"My computer."

Kent shushed her then led the way to the kitchen where piles of broken dishes and cups were scattered on the ground. Utensils had been dumped on the counter tops. Most of the food in the pantry was on the ground. Even the refrigerator hadn't been spared. One door was open and carrots, mushrooms, and tomatoes were on the floor in front of it.

"The map!" Claire rushed to the freezer. While she dug around, Kent made a quick sweep of the master bedroom.

When he returned to the kitchen, Claire was kneeling in front of the open freezer door.

"They found the map."

Chapter 30

KENT CALLED ETHAN AND WITHIN THIRTY minutes of their arrival home, the place swarmed with cops. Claire sat on the back porch rocking in the rocking chair while the authorities did what their jobs. Kent and Ethan spoke with Ben who was at his house all evening taking care of Sarah. He hadn't noticed anything, and Jill was in Dallas. No fingerprints were found.

As best as Claire could tell, the only items stolen were her laptop and the map. She'd have to clean the place before she could determine if anything else was missing. Grateful that she stored the work she did with her clients and her pictures of Eddie in the cloud, she was still in a state of disbelief.

Once her kitchen and bedroom had been cleared, she split her time between keeping hot coffee going and cleaning. The kitchen was fairly easy because most of the things on the floor were trash. Likewise with the bedroom. Every piece of clothing that was on the floor, plus anything that even looked like the intruder manhandled, went into the laundry room to be washed. By the time dawn broke on Sunday, her bedroom and the kitchen were clean and reeked of disinfectant.

As it grew light outside, the remaining officers spread out to inspect the grounds. They found that a portion of the side fence at the front corner of the property had been cut.

Claire was cleaning the living room when Kent and Ethan walked inside. One look at Kent's face and Claire set down the broom and joined them in the kitchen.

Kent grasped her hands. "We found where they came in."

"They?"

Kent nodded. "They cut part of the barbed wire fence at the southeast corner at the front of the property and we were able to identify two sets of footprints." He paused, glancing at Ethan before re-focusing on Claire. "And Bear is missing."

Claire's lower lip quivered and tears slid down her cheeks. "Missing? Did they take him?"

"We don't know. They might have secured him somewhere to keep him quiet."

She let Kent comfort her briefly before she pulled back and sniffed. Anger built and threatened to take over. "This is really pissing me off." She was huffing as she turned to the coffeepot and poured another cup for herself. Looking at both men, she raised the pot in question. Both nodded, so Claire poured them each a cup.

"We need to talk." Kent suggested they sit at the dining table.

Once settled, Claire asked, "Now that they have the map, they'll leave me alone right?"

Ethan shook his head. "Doubtful. They may think you have a copy. At the very least, you've seen it."

"Your computer is password-protected, right?"

Claire looked at Kent and nodded. "Yes."

"That doesn't mean they won't be able to access it or the data that's on it."

"True, Ethan, but most of my stuff is in the cloud and not on the hard drive."

Kent asked, "What about the program Grace gave you and your initial findings with respect to Boerne?"

"I kept everything on the flash drive she gave me, the program as well as what I found when I overlayed the treasure map with Boerne." She pulled the flash drive out of her pocket. "The only thing I'll need is another laptop or computer."

"I can help you there." Ethan reached for a computer bag on the floor next to his chair. He opened it and pulled out a laptop. "Grace said it's a little old but works well and you're welcome to it until you get another one or yours is recovered. She also said that she's taking you to the Bistro for lunch tomorrow, no excuses, and to meet her at eleven-thirty."

Claire got up and walked over to Ethan, leaning down to give him a hug then a peck on the cheek before returning to her chair. "The hug is for Grace and the kiss is for you. Thank you both." She picked up her cup and took a sip of coffee. "So it's a race now since they have the map."

"But they don't have the program so we're a couple of steps ahead of them. We just need to figure out who 'they' are."

"I have a list in my mind."

Both men looked at Claire.

"What? I've been watching people and I'm able to deduce things."

Kent nodded. "Do tell."

"Jill and Ben, Jackie, Deputy Hanson…"

"You added Deputy Hanson?"

She looked at Kent, blushing. "Yeah, I included him out of anger more than anything. He's not a nice man." She sighed. "But he's also not really a suspect."

Ethan nodded. "Why Jackie? Jealousy can be a strong motive, but is it enough?"

Claire shrugged. "Maybe. And I honestly don't believe Jill and Ben are involved. Well, I don't want to believe it. After what happened with Eddie, though…" Claire trailed off. "This isn't really a list at all, is it?"

"We've already been trying to find connections between everyone, especially the connection to Robert Smalley. We're also investigating him, of course, since Ian Smalley is his great-grandfather. He's in Dallas but could easily direct his minions, whoever they are, from there." Ethan stretched his arms over his head.

Kent nodded. "My friend in Dallas left me a message yesterday morning, said he had information and needed to talk. I tried calling him back before we went to dinner but missed him." His phone buzzed and he pulled it out of his pocket. "Speaking of…" Excusing himself, he walked to the living room.

Claire was offering Ethan more coffee when Kent returned.

His mouth was set in a grim line and he was pale. He looked first at Claire then at Ethan. He swallowed a couple of times before speaking. "Cole was killed in a car accident last night."

Chapter 31

"Oh Kent! I'm so sorry!" Claire was out of her seat in an instant and walked straight into his arms, wrapping him in a hug.

"I need to speak with Ethan."

Claire nodded and pulled back. "I'm going to clean the living room."

She attacked the room, moving like a tornado. She was afraid of what would happen if she stopped and allowed herself to feel. She was vacuuming the rug when Kent touched her arm. Gasping, she jumped and looked behind her.

"I'm sorry for startling you." Kent looked exhausted. "I'm going to take a quick shower then drive to Dallas. I need to be there to retrace Cole's steps. A phone call isn't enough."

"How long will you be gone?"

"I'll be back tomorrow." He took her hands in his and squeezed. "Ethan and I spoke with Ben. He and the ranch hands will work in the immediate area all day so someone will be close. I also called Deputy Hanson and he's on his way over here." When she opened her mouth to object, he held up his hand. "I realize he's not your favorite person but I want someone here to protect you until I return."

"So he'll be inside the house? Do I feed him? I mean, how does this work?" Claire was unnerved, rattling off the first things that came to mind.

"He'll more than likely bring some things to snack on but dinner would be a nice gesture. He will patrol the immediate area during the day and can sleep on the couch tonight. You can still have lunch with Grace tomorrow, but Deputy Hanson will go with you."

Claire's shoulders sagged and she blinked rapidly, fighting tears.

Kent lifted her chin and looked into her eyes. The depth of feeling she saw made her breath catch. "We're going to find whoever is doing this, but knowing that you're safe will ease my mind." A small smile crossed his lips. "You're exhausted. Take a shower then go to bed. Ethan said he'd stay here until Hanson arrives." He kissed her softly.

"I'll be fine but please be careful. You're tired too and Dallas is a long way away."

"I'll call you later tonight." He turned Claire toward her bedroom and gave her a little push. "Go."

With a last look in his direction, she picked up her bag and the laptop, then walked into her room and closed the door.

She awoke slowly, jumping out of bed when she realized that she'd slept seven hours. She quickly dressed and brushed her hair, then walked into the kitchen, hesitating when she realized that Deputy Hanson was sitting at the dining table drinking water and speaking in low tones on the phone. He hung up and stood as soon as she entered.

"Deputy Hanson, hello." She continued into the kitchen.

"Ms. St. John." He walked to the island. "I hope you were able to rest."

Claire nodded. "I'm actually surprised I slept as long as I did."

"Lieutenant Marshall introduced me to your foreman and ranch hands when I arrived. The breach in the fence was repaired today and everything outside is secure. I instructed Ben to notify me of any deliveries before allowing anyone inside the property. He told me two deliveries were scheduled for today, one already arrived with no issues. A late delivery is expected within the next couple of hours. Ben will call when the truck arrives at the front gate."

"Thank you for that update, Deputy." He continued to stand there, fiddling with the cap on his water bottle. Claire frowned. "Is there anything else?"

"Call me Jeremy, please." He glanced down at his hands briefly before returning his gaze to hers. "I...I just want to apologize for my behavior during the early part of this investigation. I was rude and it was uncalled for."

Claire's chin raised as her head tilted back slightly. "Thank you for that...Jeremy." She glanced toward the refrigerator "I'm starving and I'm going to make dinner. Would you like to join me?"

"I appreciate that, ma'am, but I'm dining with Ben and his wife tonight."

"It's Claire."

He nodded. "If you'll excuse me, I need to make my rounds before dinner and that delivery. Make sure to lock the door tonight. Rest assured that you're safe."

"You won't be back? I can have the sofa ready for you."

"I'd prefer staying in my truck...I don't plan on sleeping much tonight."

"By the way, I'm meeting a friend for lunch at the Bistro tomorrow at eleven-thirty. I plan to leave here at eleven."

"I'll be ready to go and will follow you there."

"Good night Jeremy."

Chapter 32

THE BLUSTERY, RAINY DAY COULDN'T DAMPEN Claire's spirits. Joining her friend for lunch was the best therapy.

Claire arrived at Barkley's a few minutes early, beating Grace. Deputy Hanson left to grab some lunch, telling her not to leave the bistro until he returned. Rolling her eyes, she had begrudgingly agreed.

She waved to Gina who was serving a couple by the window. Every table was occupied so she proceeded to the smaller room in the back, dodging a busboy who raced past her carrying a load of dishes. All tables and booths in the back were empty except for one. Four women sitting together in a booth stopped talking as soon as Claire walked in. She acknowledged them then chose a booth on the opposite side of the room, noticing how their heads immediately converged, occasionally glancing at her. Claire sighed. *Maybe one day I won't be the subject of all the gossip.*

"Boy are you a sight for sore eyes."

Claire smiled and stood back up to hug Grace. "I could say the same."

They slid into the booth and Gina walked over to them, handing each a menu. "Good morning ladies. Iced tea today?" When both nodded she left, returning moments later with their drinks. "I'll be back in a few to take your orders."

Grace leaned forward, speaking in a low voice. "Ethan told me some of what's going on. Are you okay? Do you need help cleaning? Have you had a chance to use the program I gave you?"

"That's so sweet of you but I've got the clean-up under control. And your laptop was a godsend. Thank you. As for the program, I compared the map to Boerne, and it could be the right town, although a few things don't match. I started comparing it to Austin last night. I needed to keep my mind occupied. This is like a waking nightmare, one thing after another. I keep wondering how much more I can take."

"Oh hon, you are strong, don't forget that." Grace squeezed her hand.

They were interrupted by Gina who took their orders and let them know that Maggie was going to join them in a few minutes.

"I'm just grateful Eddie isn't here."

"No kidding." A movement caught her eye and Grace looked up to observe Jackie entering the bistro. Waving her over, they exchanged a few pleasantries before Jackie excused herself saying she was meeting a friend. She walked to the table just beyond their booth and sat down.

Without missing a beat, Grace returned to their conversation. "Have you spoken to Kent?"

"Last night. He met with the officers who were on duty Saturday night. He didn't give me any details, just said he's trying to find out what his friend wanted to tell him. He was planning to work on that this morning and he's going to Judson Development as well. He'll be back tonight."

"Well, lookie-loo, my two favorite ladies." Maggie's voice reverberated in the room as she swept in and sat down next to Claire. Maggie was an entity unto herself and had more energy than most people.

"How ya' doing hon? All settled in at the ranch? I haven't seen you since William's funeral. That was ages ago. I miss seeing you regularly when you were right across the street. Now you're a big hoity-toity gal running a ranch."

"Oh please."

Maggie cackled. When she stopped, Claire said, "I want to pick your brain about something."

"Pick away, although there's not much brain left."

Conversation stopped as Gina arrived with their food.

Grace inhaled, a dreamy look on her face. "Hmmm… Everything is better with bacon, breakfast or lunch, it doesn't matter."

"Agreed." Claire sank her teeth into her BLT sandwich with avocado slices. "I miss eating here. I miss you too."

"Oh you. Now, what do you want to talk to me about?"

Claire leaned closer to Maggie and whispered. "I'm curious about the San Antonio & Aransas Pass railway. Part of it is now the trail that crosses Blanco Road, right?"

"Yep, it's called the Old Number Nine trail. The railway initially went from San Antonio to Corpus Christi but they brought it to Boerne in the eighteen-eighties and it went through Comfort and on up to Kerrville."

Claire popped a potato chip in her mouth. "Was that always the route?"

Maggie straightened her back. "Why are we all scrunched up? It's doing a number on this old back."

"Because we don't want anyone to hear." Grace shushed her.

Maggie lowered her voice. "Back in the eighteen-fifties, a family, last name Johns, bought a substantial amount of land just west of here. It was on the west side of what is now Johns Road and continued for many miles. The senior Johns, I can't remember his name, wanted to run a cattle ranch, but he was also convinced there was gold beneath the land."

"More tea ladies?"

As she was filling their glasses, Claire glanced at Jackie, who still slouched at her table. When Jackie perked up and looked toward the entrance, Claire looked over her shoulder.

Deputy Hanson's eyes roamed the room, pausing briefly when he looked at Jackie before continuing until he spotted Claire. He walked to their table.

"Deputy Hanson?"

"I've been called to Tapatio Springs regarding the other case I'm working. I should be back in about forty minutes. Stay here until I return." Without waiting for a response, he turned and left.

Claire let out an exaggerated sigh. "He's my security until Kent gets home."

"You're kidding." Grace watched the deputy leave.

Maggie pursed her lips and leaned toward Claire. "Are things that serious?"

Claire waved away her concern. "Just a precaution. I'd rather talk more about the Johns family."

"Yes, like how do you know about them, Maggie?" Grace leaned over the table.

"My great-grandma was courted by Johns Jr."

"You're kidding!" Claire was equally enthralled with the story.

"Her daddy, my great-great-granddaddy started the saloon here and was friends with Johns senior. Anyway, in the late sixties the SAAP railroad was looking to extend the railway from San Antonio to Boerne. They decided to run the rail a little north of what is now interstate ten going right through the Johns property. They even laid part of the path of the rail there, said they were allowed to under em...em...what's it called when the government takes over land?"

"Eminent domain," said Claire.

"Yeah that. Well, Johns senior threw a fit. He said they couldn't build on his property because of the mine."

Claire's jaw went slack.

"My friend couldn't make it after all so I'm going to take off."

Everyone jumped when Jackie interrupted them.

"Oh no. Are you sure you wouldn't like to join us?"

"Thanks Grace but I'm going to pass. Not in the mood anymore."

"Let's plan to catch up after Thanksgiving. I'll call you later this week to set something up."

Jackie nodded. "Y'all have a great day and happy Thanksgiving!"

As soon as she left, the three huddled together again. Grace frowned. "I'm confused. A mine?"

"Yes, Johns senior was so sure there was gold on his land he dug a mine in the early eighteen-sixties, worked on it for years. It ran below part of his land and, unbeknownst to the town, encroached into Boerne all the way to the square. When the city found out, he was fined and ordered to close the part that was outside of his property."

"Did he ever find gold?"

Maggie shook her head as she looked at Grace. "Nah, that was an expensive fool's errand." She paused and took a sip of water. "SAAP, however, checked the area and realized that the weight of the train would not be supported with a mine underneath even if filled in. So they moved to where the trail exists today. They say that the old man kept that little path for years afterward to stick it to 'em."

Shaking her head, Maggie sighed. "The ranch encompassed what today is the middle school and everything south to the interstate then west quite a few miles. The inn at the square still has some of the tunnels." She sighed. "The ranch was handed down to his son who gambled it away in less than five years. Thank goodness my great-grandma didn't end up with that loser."

"Wow, that's an amazing story Maggie." Grace took a sip of her drink.

Claire's mind raced.

She wouldn't need to compare the map to Austin or any other town. The treasure was in Boerne and it was in the old mine Johns senior built. She was sure of it.

Chapter 33

CLAIRE REACHED FOR HER BAG. "I'VE got to go."

"What? You're not even done with your lunch." Grace pouted.

"I'm sorry I can't explain right now. Thanks for lunch Grace. I'll call you later."

Maggie scrambled out of the booth, as fast as her old bones would allow her, so Claire could get out.

"Thanks. I'll be back soon, I promise." Giving Maggie a quick hug, she hurried out of the bistro. It was still raining hard and Deputy Hanson was nowhere to be found. Claire shook her head. "Like I'm going to wait here in the rain…"

Claire hopped in her car. She was shaking from the excitement and wanted to get home so she could call Kent. He was probably in meetings, but she hoped he'd be heading back soon.

She decided to make a quick stop at HEB for groceries. She stopped at the light and was gazing out the window when she spotted Deputy Hanson inside the bakery cafe across the street.

Wasn't he supposed to be in Tapatio Springs?

She was still watching him when Jackie walked from the back of the bakery and sat down next to him. He pulled her close and kissed her.

What the-?

The driver behind her tapped on his horn. She glanced toward the bakery as she drove through the intersection. Even though she was in the right lane and a car in the left lane partially blocked her, she still sunk down until she was beyond the intersection. They seemed to be too involved with each other to have noticed her.

When she exited the grocery store, it was pouring. The sound of the rain pounding on her car roof was deafening as she drove home. She soon forgot about everything except focusing on the road and the deteriorating driving conditions. It took her more than an hour to get home and her mood has soured by the time she arrived.

She pulled behind the house to park close to the rear door. Deputy Hanson was waiting for her on the back porch.

"I told you to wait for me." His tone was angry.

Shoving groceries into his hands she grabbed what was left and hurried inside. They set the groceries on the island.

Claire glared at him. "I'm not a prisoner, Jeremy. You weren't there when I was ready to go and it was pouring. I drove to HEB for groceries before coming home. Middle of the day? Crowded grocery store? I wasn't in danger. Now if you'll excuse me, I'm dripping wet and need to change." Without waiting for a reply, she turned and stomped into her bedroom, shutting the door behind her.

She dried off and put on clean clothes before putting her hair in a ponytail. Reaching into her bag, she tried calling Kent. He didn't answer, so she left him a vague message. She slipped the phone in the pocket of her leggings and walked back into the kitchen. Deputy Hanson was no longer in the house, for which she was extremely pleased.

She'd just finished putting away the food and was wiping the water off the counter when her phone rang.

"Claire, it's Kent. I'm okay but I was in an accident outside of Waco…"

"Oh God! Are you sure you're all right?" She wandered to the front window and stared outside as she listened to him explain what happened.

"The brakes gave out and I slid off the road. The rain didn't help."

Flashbacks of Michael's car accident flew through her mind.

"I didn't want you to get the news from Ethan or anyone else, and I need to tell you something. Are you home?"

"Yes, I got home a while ago. How are you going to get back? Should I drive to Waco and pick you up?"

"No, I'm getting a rental car and will head back soon. Claire, you need to be careful around Jackie…"

"That's part of my news. Jackie and Jeremy were at the bakery. They're clearly an item." Before he could respond to that revelation, she added, "And I figured out where the treasure is. It's really quite clever."

Kent paused, and his tone changed, deepening his voice. "Get out of the house, Claire, now. Go to Ethan's."

"Hang up the phone, Claire." Claire jumped at the sound of the voice behind her.

Turning around, Jeremy stood two paces away…and he was pointing a gun at her.

Chapter 34

"I said hang up." He growled, taking a step toward her.

Claire ended the call and backed up. "It's done. The call ended."

He reached over and snatched the phone from her hand. Slipping it into his pocket, he motioned with the gun for her to sit on the sofa.

She walked to the sofa while keeping her eyes on Jeremy. "What's going on Jeremy?" She sat on the edge.

"Don't play coy." Squinting, he walked behind the other sofa across from Claire and turned to watch her, periodically waving his gun up and down.

Claire sat placidly and waited. Inside, she was shaking with the effort not to show her fear.

"Waiting, waiting, waiting. That's all I've been doing these past months with no returns. I'm sick of it." He was pacing.

"Sick of what?"

Jeremy whirled on her. "Sick of the status quo. Sick of getting nowhere at the Sheriff's Office while everyone gets promoted over me. Sick of taking orders from the lieutenant, not to mention that blithering bitch." He was breathing erratically as he paced.

"That's not a pleasant thing to say about Kent, or Jackie for that matter."

His eyes widened, but then narrowed as he fixed her with a stare that sent shivers up her spine. "Shut. Up."

Claire's stomach did a few somersaults.

"I wanted to move fast, but slow was her preference. After a year I was done waiting. That's why William had to go." Claire gasped and covered her mouth. "So I took matters into my own hand to speed things along and it worked." He chuckled, a coarse evil sound.

Jeremy killed William.

Claire swallowed back the rising bile. "How could you kill that sweet man?"

"Don't be naive. That treasure today is worth millions. I thought for sure the trunk would have the map but nooooo, he hid it. Imagine my surprise when I discovered that you found the map, and you just confirmed that you know where the treasure is located." He laughed at her shock. "Did you think I missed that last comment you made to your lover?"

Before he could say anything more, his phone rang. "Yeah I'm here. And wait until you hear what I found out. The code is one-zero-six-one." He dialed another number. "Good news. She says she found the treasure." He listened to the person on the other end. "I'll text you the location as soon as this bitch tells me." He hung up and returned his gaze to Claire, as he drummed his fingers on the sofa. Minutes passed.

Claire shifted in her seat. "Why kill Lenny?"

No response.

"Why involve Jackie?"

"He didn't involve me. I brought him in on this." Claire gasped and turned her head to watch Jackie as she sauntered into the room, pulling off her beanie cap.

Claire stared at the beanie cap. "You killed Lenny!"

"With Jeremy's help." She walked over to him.

Grabbing her by the waist, he hauled her close for a kiss. When the kiss ended, she turned her head as Jeremy nuzzled her neck, watching how Claire responded. Laughing, she playfully pushed out of Jeremy's arms. When she faced Claire, her face had contorted to one of pure hatred and malice. Claire sunk back on the couch.

"Do you know what it feels like to give and give and give and never receive accolades of any kind? I intentionally ran into William at the store so that we could become acquainted and he would eventually trust me enough to bring me into his fold. I slaved for him for more than a year, picking up his groceries, dropping off laundry, even picking up around here. He relied on me but not once did he invite me to stay. Not once did he give me a hug to thank me for all that I did for him."

Her voice rose in volume and pitch. "And twenty-five-thousand in the will for a trip? Are you kidding me? Then you come along and suddenly you're the daughter he never had." Unable to stand still any longer, she paced. "He deserved to die. And Jeremy," she squeezed his arm as she passed him, "…was right to take things up a notch or two." She giggled.

"So many people before you have tried and failed to find the treasure." Claire was disgusted by Jackie's callousness.

Jackie wagged a finger at her. "They didn't have the map, did they? Neither did we, until recently anyway." Her eyes roamed the room before glancing at the office that was still in disarray. "Looks like you're making good progress cleaning up." She snickered.

"She knows where the treasure is."

Jackie's eyes narrowed as she studied Claire. "Where is it? And don't try any delaying tactics. Your boyfriend won't get home anytime soon. We made sure of that."

Claire swallowed.

They tampered with his car…?

"Where. Is. It?" Jackie's agitation was growing.

When Claire didn't respond, Jackie moved quickly and slapped her on the face snapping her head to the side. "I will ask just one more time before I tell Jeremy to put a bullet in her head."

"Then you'd never find it."

"We have the map, eventually we'd find it. But not before killing your son and aunt."

Claire's eyes shot to Jeremy and she paled.

He chuckled. "Do you honestly believe that flying them out of state would keep them safe? How long do you think it would take me to find them?"

Claire clasped her hands together until her knuckles were white. She refocused on Jackie. "I don't understand how you got involved in this."

"She's a little slow." Jeremy's tone was mocking.

Jackie sneered. "Because Robert Smalley is my grandfather, you dimwit. He sent me here, and he deserves restitution."

Chapter 35

Jackie leaned down until she was nose-to-nose with Claire. "Tell me where the treasure is." Claire hesitated. "Now!"

"It's in the old Johns mine."

"I overheard you talking about the railroad and you mentioned the mine before I left." She stood and walked over to Jeremy. "Why there?"

"Because it matches the middle Xs on the map and Billy Miner would have seen the irony of putting the treasure in a mine."

Jackie glanced at Jeremy who shrugged.

"Stay put." He and Jackie walked into the kitchen and whispered to each other.

Returning, Jackie crossed her arms and looked down at Claire. "So where's the mine?"

"The tunnels supposedly began where the middle school on Johns Road is."

Jackie barked a laugh. "You mean I've been working on top of it? That's rich."

"The mine ran to the Square according to Maggie." Claire's voice was barely audible as she thought of the danger Eddie and Jen might be in.

Jeremy snapped his fingers. "The inn has tunnels."

"How do you know this?" Jackie looked at him in surprise.

"The first case I worked on involved items in the inn's shed that were stolen. That's when I first learned about them."

Jackie sneered. "Enough of this chit chat. It's getting dark."

How would Kent find her if she went with them? "Where are we going?"

Jeremy tugged her off the sofa. "Shut up. You'll go where we tell you to." He put Claire in handcuffs. "She'll ride with me so I can keep her in check. Follow me when I pull to the front."

After a detour to shop for supplies at the local big box hardware store, they arrived at the backside of the inn. Jeremy had insisted that Jackie drive them in her car, so she drove while Jeremy sat in back with Claire. The warm weather and rain had created a blanket of fog. Claire fidgeted next to Jeremy.

The rear of the hotel where the storage shed was located was deathly quiet.

Jeremy directed Jackie to park between the shed and a row of bushes and unbuckled his belt. "I'll be right back." He opened the door. Stepping out, he quickly closed the car door and disappeared in the rain.

Claire leaned forward. "All the tools and paraphernalia you just bought? You don't really expect to find the treasure, do you? The owners of the inn have surely explored the tunnels over the years."

"Shut up!" Jackie spun around in the front seat and glared at her.

Claire hoped to raise doubt in Jackie while Bonnie and Clyde were separated. "What's the plan? Are we going to stay in the tunnels twenty-four-seven until the treasure is found? Two women and a man? What are we going to eat or drink? Do we get to sleep at all? If I knew I was going to be working in a mine, I would have changed my clothes. You probably should have done the same."

"I said shut up!" Jackie glanced down at the capri jeans and T-shirt she was wearing.

Jeremy returned. "We'll unload the car quickly then park the car two blocks over." He was talking to Jackie, but he was glaring at Claire. "Keep your mouth shut."

Jackie exited the car while Jeremy opened the passenger door and yanked Claire out by the handcuffs. Tripping as he pulled her out, she fell to her knees and cried out.

"Quiet. Get up. We need to go."

Scrambling to her feet and trying to gain her balance, she limped to the back where Jackie was pulling out shovels, a pick, buckets and bags of supplies.

Jeremy removed the handcuffs. "Don't try anything."

Claire rubbed her wrists.

The three of them walked to the shed. Dropping her load inside, Jackie left to move the car while Jeremy turned on a flashlight. Claire scowled when she observed how packed it was inside the shed. Shelving stuffed with bins and boxes lined both sides. She identified bins with Christmas decorations by their labels, but the dim light prevented her from reading others. Jeremy shift uncomfortably. His shoulders were so broad that they brushed the bins on each side.

With only the narrow beam of light, Claire felt as though the room was closing in on her.

Jeremy pushed her down the aisle, following closely behind. The two shovels that she carried clanked against each other and the plastic bags hanging from her arms bumped against her hips with every step.

They approached the end of the shed and a wooden door. She stopped when she reached it and looked behind her. Jeremy just stared at her, waiting.

A creak of the shed door announced Jackie's return. Plastic bags rustled as she made her way toward them. Instead of a flashlight, Jackie wore a hard hat with a small light on it, leaving her hands free. The dim light bounced up and down with every step she took.

Jeremy squeezed past Claire and yanked the wooden door open. He flipped on the switch and meager lighting from a single bulb illuminated the stairwell. Grinning, he headed down the wooden stairs. Jackie shoved Claire forward and closed the door behind them.

Chapter 36

CLAIRE ATTEMPTED TO TAMP DOWN HER mounting hysteria by talking.

"Boy, we'd better find that treasure before Thanksgiving. Decorating for Christmas begins the day after." No response from Jeremy or Jackie, who nudged her forward. "I sure hope I don't have to go to the bathroom soon."

The stairs creaked and groaned with each step and the pace was slow. The tension was thick making it hard to breathe, but Claire kept up her one-sided conversation. Twice she almost missed a step since she couldn't hold onto the only railing. She moved to the side without the rail so she could use her shoulder to help support her. With each step down, the air grew a little mustier.

They finally reached the bottom and Jackie pushed past her, growling, "I'm sick of your voice, Claire. Shut up!" Jeremy had already turned on the light which wasn't much brighter than the stairwell.

Claire took a few steps inside then turned a full circle. They were in a rectangular room, more storage from the look of things. A hodgepodge of items were scattered about—a rocker, a headboard, a couple of dining chairs, even a stuffed deer—all coated in dust. More shelves lined three walls and had more boxes on them.

Claire snickered. "Why wouldn't the owners just throw this stuff away? It's been down here for ages. And I hate to tell you, Jeremy, but there's no tunnel. The opening must be somewhere else."

Jeremy walked to one of the shelves on the side and pushed it away from the wall revealing another door. He opened it then turned to them with a triumphant look on his face.

"How...?" Jackie rushed over to look inside.

"One of the employees told me about it when I worked on that case. She was a cute thing." He turned to the door, missing the look of revulsion on Jackie's face.

Claire didn't miss it though, nor did she miss the opportunity. Dropping her stuff, she ran to the stairwell and made it up two steps before Jeremy grabbed her ponytail and yanked her back down. Claire screamed as she fell to the ground. Rolling over, she shrank back when Jeremy leaned over her.

"Try that again, bitch, and I'll kill you. Now get up and move."

Claire scrambled to her feet, wincing in pain as she rubbed the back of her head. She wiped her hands on her leggings then realized it was a fruitless effort as she was covered in dust. Picking up her load, she walked over to where Jeremy and Jackie were waiting.

Claire donned the hat Jackie handed her and flipped on the light.

Without another word, they entered the tunnel, Jeremy in the lead followed by Claire, and Jackie bringing up the rear. The tunnel was all dirt, a little wider than the staircase. It was high enough that she could stand without bending over but Jeremy was too tall and had to stoop. The earthy smell was strong.

She couldn't tell how long they walked but Jeremy finally stopped at a Y. A trickle of fresh air blew from the right. She sucked it into her lungs.

Jackie did the same. "Where is that air coming from?"

Jeremy glanced at them. "Once I found out about the tunnels, I decided to explore them. The air is coming from a small opening around the corner that leads out. It's hidden under a bridge, too narrow to crawl into or out of. Luckily the managers at the inn only lock the outer door of the shed with a combination lock, even after the burglary." He shook his head. "It was easy enough to come back in and explore. Had I known the treasure was here…. This way." He turned left and continued walking.

Claire lost track of time walking in the dark with only their head lamps to guide them. The quiet was eerie, broken only by the sound of their footsteps in the dirt, Jeremy's breathing, and Jackie's whispered complaints loud enough for only Claire to hear.

The tunnel narrowed and the ceiling dropped, forcing Jeremy to almost double over. Even Claire and Jackie had to stoop. She was about to complain when it opened into a square room the size of an average bedroom. Framed at the top by wooden beams along the walls, columns at each corner supported it.

Jeremy dropped his supplies and straightened, rubbing his lower back. "This is as far as it goes and this is where the real mining tunnel begins."

Chapter 37

Claire set her things down as she took in the room. The two side walls were packed dirt. The back wall had loose dirt and some had slid down to form a pile on the ground. Jeremy knelt by three lanterns as he installed batteries in them.

"You've got to be kidding!" She laughed at Jeremy. "You didn't think this through very well."

Rushing over to her, he grabbed her by her shoulders and slammed her against the wall.

Gasping, she stared at Jeremy, her heart racing. His face contorted in rage and his eyes were wild.

"I wouldn't hurt her if you expect her to dig." Jackie looked around the room in disgust.

Jeremy's face and stance relaxed although his breathing was still erratic. Letting go of Claire, he turned and picked up a shovel. "Good point." He thrust the shovel at her. Her fingers automatically grasped the handle. "You go first." He pointed to the wall with the loose dirt.

She walked past him. "What makes you believe there's more tunnel behind this dirt or that this is even the right place to dig? And how long do we dig before you realize that nothing is back there?"

He handed her a mask and eye goggles. "That's for me to worry about. Just dig."

Claire faced the wall, donning the mask and goggles. Placing her foot on top of the shovel head, she pressed down into the dirt. It was still loose and easily filled the shovel. She twisted to the side, the shovel of dirt in her hand. She raised her eyebrows and the shovel, questioning Jeremy without saying a word.

"Jackie, get the two buckets and put one by Claire."

Frowning, Jackie did as told. As soon as it was full she placed the second bucket by Claire and stepped aside, watching as Jeremy picked up the full bucket then disappeared into the tunnel returning a moment later with the bucket now empty. Every time a bucket was filled, he'd empty it somewhere in the tunnel.

The two worked in silence until Claire finally stopped. "I need a break." She stood up to ease her back. "I don't suppose you thought to buy gloves?" Jeremy's look was her answer. "Why am I not surprised?"

"Shut up and keep digging."

"I said I need a break."

Jeremy pointed to the corner. "Sit over there." His gaze turned to Jackie. "Your turn."

Without saying a word, Jackie picked up the shovel and began digging.

They worked for what seemed like hours, Claire and Jackie alternating with the shoveling. Jeremy allowed a water break every hour. Sweat was pouring off Claire. She had long since discarded her sweatshirt. Her hands had multiple blisters that stung and were slippery with sweat making it difficult to shovel, and her arm and leg muscles were screaming in protest.

She no longer sat down when Jackie took over the digging because she didn't think she'd be able to get back up. So she just leaned against the wall waiting for her turn.

During one break, Claire gratefully dropped the shovel and pulled off her mask and goggles. Despite using the goggles, dust and dirt still bothered her eyes. She reached down for a bottle of water and twisted it open, wincing a little in pain. She tipped the bottle and drank the tepid water, relishing the wetness as it slid down her dusty throat.

She looked at their progress and grimaced. The dent they had made was obvious but it all just felt pointless, a stab in the dark.

Evidently Jackie felt the same. "I'm done." She walked over to Jeremy and placed her raw palm against his cheek. "This is a waste of time. That treasure could be anywhere down here. It could be completely buried with no more tunnels to find." She kissed him gently on his lips. "I'm tired. I'm hungry. Despite my grandfather's obsession with the treasure, this isn't worth it anymore."

"Aww, Jackie." Jeremy grabbed her head and stared at her as he rammed a knife to the hilt under her ribs.

Her eyes widened and she gurgled, blood dribbling out of her mouth and down her chin.

When he released her head, she fell to the ground.

Chapter 38

SHOCK HELD CLAIRE IMMOBILE. HER MOUTH opened and closed but no sound came out.

"You ruined my surprise for her."

Claire turned toward the tunnel entrance. "Jill?"

Dressed in black jeans, a black T-shirt, and black boots, she didn't look anything like Ben's wife. Claire rubbed her forehead, trying to make sense of a world that had tilted.

"About time you got here." Jeremy stepped over Jackie's body and approached Jill. Leaning down, he kissed her then smacked her on her bottom.

Jill laughed, a full-bodied laugh that grated on Claire's nerves. "I had to drive back from Dallas although I've been here since you dumped that last bucket of dirt. Kind of fun watching your little routine. You'd get it done faster if you did this yourself, though."

"You're probably right. I just didn't want that one sneaking off. She already tried once. Figured if she was working, she'd be too tired to try escaping." He picked up the shovel.

Jill sauntered further into the room, looking at Claire for the first time. "Don't look at me like that."

"Like what? I'm trying to understand what's going on. What about Ben, Sarah?"

Jill sniffed. "Ben served a purpose, a means to an end. So did Sarah. She was a welcome diversion from my tedious life. William loved her so it kept me closer to him." She giggled. "Her fall at the park was the distraction I needed, by the way."

"What?"

"Don't be obtuse." She patted Jeremy on his butt as he walked by with a bucket of dirt. "Jeremy was very helpful that day."

Claire paled at the implication.

Jill's head tilted back slightly and she sneered at Jackie's body. "I had to watch my niece…" she used the toe of her boot to nudge Jackie's dead body, "…grow up being adored by our fathers." Her tone changed, turning bitter, as she strode to the far wall and back. "But for the simple fact that he raped his maid which resulted in a pregnancy, I could have been the exalted one. As it was, my father ignored me and only tolerated my mother after that."

As she spoke, Jeremy continued to shovel, fill a bucket, and leave to empty it before returning and repeating the process.

Claire watched Jill. "Robert Smalley is your father?"

Her lip curled with contempt. "He asked for my help long before he sent his granddaughter down here. He found out years ago that William was a descendant of Billy Miner and wanted someone to get close to him. I agreed only if I received a fat allowance to buy all the things I'd need to succeed. I finally received what was due to me. Manipulating Ben was easy enough and it was the quickest way to get close to William."

Eyes looking off in the distance, she laughed at the memories. "I had him proposing a month after I intro-duced myself to him at the post office. He couldn't get enough of me." Stepping closer to Claire, she continued to ramble. "I didn't plan on getting pregnant but then again, I didn't plan on being married that long. Ranching...such a boring life, not at all like life in the city. Jeremy changed all of that, made things bearable. It was so easy to make up excuses to get out of the house and meet him."

The corner of her mouth lifted in a semblance of a smile as she glanced at Jeremy who, at the moment, was removing his shirt. "My father sent Jackie down from Dallas a couple years ago. He had the nerve to suggest that I wasn't moving fast enough." Back and forth she paced. "I'll kill him before I let him take any of the treasure."

Clair was perplexed, and her mind was spinning. "You married Ben and started a family with him just to get close to William?"

Jill shrugged. "You do whatcha gotta do." She glanced at her watch.

"What time is it?" Claire asked.

"A little after one..."

There was a clanging noise that startled both wom-en. They looked at Jeremy who was cussing. "Just hit rock with the shovel. Damn that hurt!" He dropped the shovel and rubbed his arm and elbow.

"Is that a good thing?" Jill scooted closer to Jeremy while keeping Claire in her sights.

Jeremy rolled his head a couple of times. "Right now, it just means that I hit rock." He lifted a pick from the ground and began whacking at the wall. Chips of rock flew in all directions. Claire slipped the goggles and mask back on for protection.

She wanted to ask so many more questions but the repeated pick blows to the rock made it impossible to talk. She and Jill watched Jeremy work in silence. Dazed and exhausted, she jumped when Jeremy shouted in triumph.

"Yes, yes, yes." There was a small opening in the rock and Jeremy squatted down to look through the hole. He leaned back, rocking back and forth on his toes and grinning as he turned his head toward Jill. "Looks like there's more tunnel on the other side." With renewed energy, he hopped up and used the pick to punch a bigger hole in the wall.

"Hand me the long lighter in that bag over there, Jill." He pointed to a bag near Claire.

Jill walked over and leaned down for the bag. Claire seized the moment and shoved her with all her might. Stumbling back, Jill tripped over Jackie's body and slammed into Jeremy as she screamed.

Claire half-limped, half-ran into the tunnel, racing as fast as her tired body allowed. The light from the hat she still wore illuminated the ground a foot or two in front of her. She heard Jeremy shouting and Jill crying before his footsteps sounded behind her. She glanced behind her as she rounded a corner and slammed into something.

She opened her mouth to scream but a hand covered her mouth.

"Claire it's me, Kent."

She stopped struggling and her eyes flew to his face.

Hearing the approaching footsteps, Kent shoved Claire behind him. Ethan grabbed her and motioned for her to get behind him as well. Holding his fist up, he counted to three with his fingers. When he got to three, Ethan went high aiming a spotlight around the corner and Kent went low.

"It's over Jeremy," Kent growled.

Jeremy threw a hand over his eyes and slid to a stop. "Never." When he raised his gun. Kent pumped two bullets into his chest. Jeremy toppled backward landing on the ground with a thud. Running over to him with his gun still raised, Kent kneeled down and checked his pulse.

Ethan and Claire joined Kent. Both men remained alert.

Claire whispered, "Ben's wife, Jill, is still back there. She's involved with Jeremy. Jackie is there too. She's dead."

Telling her to wait, Kent and Ethan cautiously approached the room. Claire was right behind them. No way was she going to hang out in the dark alone with a dead man.

When they walked into the cave they took in the scene, noting Jackie's body. Jill was huddled in a corner. Her lip was bloody and a bruise was developing on her cheek.

Ethan walked up to her and placed her under arrest, reading the Miranda rights to her as they walked out of the room.

Kent took one look at Claire and wrapped her in his arms. "It's over. You're safe."

The tears fell and Claire cried for William and Lenny, and she cried for herself as relief washed over her. She didn't notice when Kent sat down on the floor with her in his arms. Finally hiccoughing a few times, she sniffed and pulled back to look at Kent. "How…"

"We'll sort everything out later. Right now, I want to get you out of here."

Kent's eyes took in everything, rubbing his chin. "Unbelievable."

"Jeremy actually broke through to what might be a continuation of the tunnel when I saw the opportunity to run."

His eyebrows creeped up. "You don't say?"

Kent helped her up and they moved over to the hole. Kneeling, he picked up the lighter. The hiss of the flame as Kent flicked it on momentarily mesmerized her. Reaching his arm inside the hole, they both leaned close.

Claire gasped.

Reflecting off the flicker of the lighter's flame, gold shimmered like liquid fire.

Epilogue

Thanksgiving Day

"Mama, Mama, Mama!"

Claire lifted Eddie into her arms and held him close as she covered his face in kisses, his giggles warming her heart. Finally having enough, Eddie squirmed until she set him down. He ran inside as she turned to Kent and her aunt who were walking to the door.

"Aunt Jen." Claire pulled her aunt into a tight hug. "Thank you so much for taking such good care of Eddie and for skipping Thanksgiving with Aunt Joan."

Jen pulled away, holding Claire's hands. "Oh darlin', don't you worry about that. I'll go back to Kentucky for Christmas. We had such fun and I can't wait to tell you all about it. But first I need you to point me to the restroom. I have had to tinkle since before we left the airport." She disappeared through the door.

Claire looked at Kent. "Thank you for picking them up." She took a deep breath and let it out slowly. "I'm so happy they're here and Aunt Jen was willing to come back early. I've missed Eddie."

"Happy to do it." Kent placed his arm around her shoulder and they walked inside. "I hope the girls behaved."

"Of course they did. They're in the barn with Ben and Sarah right now. Ethan, Grace and the rest should be here soon." With the return of Eddie, they had all agreed to have Thanksgiving dinner at Claire's ranch instead of Ethan's.

They walked into the kitchen. The turkey was cooking, a large pot of water was boiling with potatoes, and a green bean casserole and a casserole with stuffing were sitting on the counter ready to go into the oven.

Eddie ran to Ginger and Louise, who had just bounced in, followed by Ben and Sarah…and Bear.

"Look who's back."

Eddie screamed in delight and raced over to Bear, wrapping him in a hug.

"Ben, what…how…?"

Ben walked over to Claire. "Clyde found him at the back of the property stuck in the barbed wire fence. He and Erwin cleaned up his cuts but his pads look pretty raw. They'll take longer to heal. Poor guy must have been wandering around trying to get home."

Claire knelt by Bear and kissed his nose. "We missed you, sweet boy." She returned to Kent's side as the girls surrounded Bear and Eddie. She closed her eyes and pressed a hand to her chest.

"Penny for your thoughts."

She looked at Kent. "I still can't believe that the nightmare is over and we're all having Thanksgiving together." So much had happened since the night in the tunnel.

Realizing that her father was going to throw her under the bus, Jill told the police everything—the endless stories of how Billy Miner swindled her family, her father's obsession with the treasure, how she was told to do whatever was necessary to get close to William.

What shocked and saddened Claire the most was when Jill described how her father ordered the hit against Kent, his friend Cole, and Michael because they were asking questions and getting too close to the truth. His instructions were only that they should look like accidents. Jill had traveled to Dallas over the weekend at her father's insistence to ensure success, as she did with Michael and Cole. To have senselessly lost Michael and almost lost Kent…her mind reeled.

Claire would never comprehend the level of greed that made Robert Smalley so intent on finding the treasure that he'd buy property under false pretenses, involve his daughter and granddaughter in his scheme, and kill innocent people.

After learning a few details, Claire had asked Kent not to relay any more information about the case. She'd heard enough and needed time to reflect and grieve.

The rest of the wall in the tunnel was knocked down. Billy Miner's treasure had been removed, inventoried, and was being stored in her lawyer's vault while the legalities were finalized. She smiled recalling how fast Clarence made it to the inn after she called.

Kent had been her constant companion since then, and she was awash with gratitude for him and for her life with her son. Knowing that it could all have been taken away was something she'd never forget.

She'd convinced Ben to stay, telling him that he and Sarah were family. He'd shared his gratitude, stating that the ranch was his home and he couldn't imagine bringing Sarah up anywhere else.

Claire shook off her recollections as the back door opened and Ethan, Grace, Jo, and Chase walked in. The chaos that ensued with Eddie running over to each for a hug made her realize, once more, how special her son was.

"We have a lot to be thankful for."

Claire turned her gaze to Kent. "I was just thinking the same thing. Come here for a minute."

Grabbing Kent's hand, she pulled him over to the fireplace. The police had recovered the trunk and it was sitting on the hearth. She studied Billy Miner's portrait that she'd re-framed, the eight-by-ten picture of William with Eddie that was leaning next to it, as well as Billy's map which she'd also framed.

Kent picked up the map. "What could the X at the top of the map mean?"

"Given what William told me, it sounded like he believed the X was this land and that Billy may have lived and buried the treasure here. He had all those holes dug, after all."

Kent shrugged. "Makes about as much sense as everything else." He placed the frame back on the mantle and turned to Claire.

"I realize that I haven't thanked you for finding me and for everything you've done."

He shook his head. "When you told me that Jackie and Jeremy were together...I was the one who ordered Jeremy to guard you."

"You can't blame yourself for that, you didn't know."

Kent sighed. "Nevertheless, it was my job to protect you…"

She placed her finger on his lips. "You put two-and-two together and called Maggie and Grace. You saved me." She scrunched her nose and punched him lightly on his arm. "So paste a smile on your face and accept my gratitude."

Kent chuckled then turned serious as he pulled her close. "I would do anything for you, Claire." He leaned down to kiss her when they were interrupted.

"Mama, Mama, Mama." Eddie ran over to them. "Hungy."

Kent and Claire laughed as Kent lifted Eddie and settled him on his shoulders. Kent danced to the kitchen causing Eddie to giggle. Claire looked at the people who had gathered, people she loved. Life was good. Life was very good.

THE END

Note from Author

If you enjoyed this novel, please leave a review.
They are so important for authors who self-publish.

Go to the book's Amazon page, scroll down to the
'Customer Reviews' section and click the 'Write a
Customer Review' button. For your convenience,
you can also click the link below:

**https://www.amazon.com/gp/product/
B0DWLZKX9P**

Thank you so much!

Getting Out of Debt Workbook

In Treasure & Treachery, you learned that Claire was a financial advisor who was creating an authenticated area on her website for her clients. Part of that authenticated area was to include a budget workbook that she planned to create.

When I was in my twenties, I ran into financial difficulties. Many years after I pulled myself out of that situation, I started writing a workbook and I finally completed it.

Turn the page to read the preface of my workbook and at the end, you'll be able to download a copy for FREE.

Take care!

Getting Out of Debt
A Practical Workbook

Preface

I'VE ALWAYS BEEN A SAVER. I'M not sure when it started, but for as far back as I can remember, I would save my allowance instead of spending it. Seeing my savings account grow was cool to me. So when I found myself, at the age of twenty six, without any savings and spending more money than I made, I was at a loss. How did I get here?

It goes without saying, as most of us can attest to, that it wasn't just one event or job or purchase (or whatever) that put me in my precarious position. Rather, it was a combination of many things.

During my last year of college, I obtained a student loan. It helped with some expenses but mostly paid for my graduation trip to Australia (what a fabulous trip that was…but that's another story). When I returned from my travels, it took me awhile (and some of my savings) to get that first job but I was eventually on my way in the world and making a modest income. I was living in southern California and having a great time.

I eventually moved back north to Stockton, California, where I earned my Real Estate license and became a Loan Officer. Selling money was easy, I was told. What better commodity to sell? This was in 1986 and the real estate market in that part of the state was good… steady. For the first 3 months, I received a small income to give me an opportunity to build relationships with real estate agents. After that, my pay was 100% commission.

Shortly after moving to Stockton, I also bought a brand new Mazda 4-door 626 sedan. I traded in my Ford Granada and didn't need any money down to get the car of my dreams (of course that meant my monthly payment was more, but I was a Loan Officer extraordinaire so no problem, right?). By the time I bought my car, I also had two important credit cards (from my point of view): Bank of America MasterCard and Nordstrom. There were a few other cards, a Visa and a couple of other department store cards. But I loved having my MasterCard (with a $5000 limit) and my Nordstrom card!

It took me two years in that job to arrive at a couple of important realizations. First, I serviced the loans really well. I was friendly and excelled in communications and in moving the loan through to approval. Second, the commodity didn't matter…I was not a salesperson. I could not get the real estate agents to give me a try and bring me their clients.

Over the course of those two years, I was supplementing my meager commission income with money from my savings account and my credit cards. By early 1988, my cards were maxed out and my bank balance was close to zero.

My Debt

Type of Debt	Monthly Pymt	Balance Due	Interest Rate
Auto Loan	~240	$16000.00	4%
BofA Mastercard	min 51	$5000.00	18%
Nordstrom	min 35	$1500.00	21%
Other Cards	~150	$5000.00	varied
Student Loan	60	$5000.00	n/a
Rent/Utilities	600	on-going	n/a
TOTAL:	**$1136.00**	**$32500.00**	

How I got here was no longer important. How to get out of the hole I dug became a priority. I had to do something, and fast.

***

Have you ever found yourself in a similar position? Are you in this dilemma now, juggling bills from month to month, wondering which ones to pay and which bills will have to wait? Do you feel like you're drowning in debt, that you'll never get out from under it all?

If so, then this might be the workbook for you. The tips and lessons outlined in the chapters that follow are intended to give you practical advice and steps that not only can help reduce and eliminate your debt, but also save money. This is not a theoretical lecture from a financial analyst or other expert telling you what to do. This workbook is written by someone who has been there, like you are now, and who pulled herself out of a mountain of debt.

Now, I am **NOT** a financial consultant nor am I telling you what to do, but I believe that the lessons and exercises that worked for me can also work for you.

Is it going to be easy? No. Will you wake up tomorrow after reading this workbook and magically be out of debt? No. It's going to take effort and dedication on your part, day in and day out. But I'm here to tell you that you can do it! You can pay off your debt, save money and enjoy a life that is not stressed due to finances. I'm living proof of that!

So what have you got to lose? If you're ready to take the next step toward your financially secure future, let's get started!

***

Get your **FREE** copy today!

If you feel that this workbook can help you get out of debt and lead to a less stressful life, click the link below. In addition to the workbook, you will also receive the files of the budget template and worksheets.

www.kadyhinojosa.com/godw

Take care and God bless!